The Sunken Town

KAREN NELSON

Sibylline
DIGITAL FIRST

Sibylline Press is dedicated to publishing the brilliant
work of women authors ages 50 and older.
www.sibyllinepress.com

Sibylline Digital First Edition

ISBN: ebook 9781960573261
ISBN: print 9781960573391
LCCN: 2024948693

Cover Design: Alicia Feltman
Book Production: Sang Kim

Sibylline
DIGITAL FIRST

To My Parents

Between every two pine trees there is a door leading to a new way of life.

John Muir

CHAPTER ONE

Claire

A missing person is not declared legally dead in Maine for seven years, but all I need is seven months. Maybe Charles Price planted the seed with his fraternity prank, maybe not, but if my plan works it will solve all my problems. If it doesn't, then I'll have to find another way to escape the Price family's control. If only I hadn't decided to spend my junior year back east as an exchange student. If only I hadn't camped out on Haskin's Hill with the Outing Club during orientation week, finding the idea quaint and romantic—full of that New England charm I'd come looking for, all red brick and white trim and green ivy. Lacrosse games, a cappella singing groups, and musty labyrinths of library stacks. If only my parents were still alive.

If only it hadn't started to rain.

I hadn't heard the rumors about the Royals yet. I didn't know the truth behind the lies. But I'm getting ahead of myself. I will do my best to stick to the truth, at least the truth as I remember it, and you can judge for yourself.

Once classes had finished for the school year, I pulled Lauren's car alongside the Outing Club shack as the last rays of afternoon sun descended over the library tower. A guy manning the inventory, who would have benefited from a bar of soap, pulled his head out of his Appalachian Trail map long enough to help me manhandle the canoe onto the roof and strap it down.

Sunrise was scheduled for 5:11 a.m. I set my alarm for 3:30 and dressed in layers of wicking fabrics. I gave one last look around my dorm room. My toiletries waited in my shower bucket next to my towel. My books fanned across my desk and night stand. Tacked to my bulletin board were pictures of friends, comic strips, and a fortune from a cookie. My bed was made and my dirty clothes were piled in my hamper. No one besides me would recognize anything was missing. I locked the door and snuck out of my dorm into the foggy darkness of pre-dawn. The pathway lamps cast islands of light that I followed to the parking lot, where the bulky shape of the canoe made the car easier to spot in the far row.

At the Lone Loon Pond campground, I eased myself under the canoe and braced, hoping to reap the benefit from all my track-team weight room squats. Balancing the craft on my shoulders, I maneuvered it from the roof of the car down onto the boat ramp, bruising my shin in the process. I looped my arms through the life jacket, grabbed the paddle, and hid Lauren's keys behind the gas-cap cover. The boat ramp disappeared into an ink-black void; the shoreline along the campground was uninhabited, and no lights shone from the camps farther around the lake. I waded into the water until the canoe floated, then settled myself on the rear seat and launched into the dark. As I paddled toward the rumored location of where the town once stood, the water lapped lightly against the boat's side. The still air hummed with crickets and a solitary loon wailed into the darkness. Water dripped from each stroke of my paddle, and I smelled pine and lake water. A light mist hung over the surface.

About a mile from shore I let the canoe drift. The sky was

starting to lighten. Stars no longer visible overhead, but dawn still half an hour away. I placed the life jacket in the bottom of the canoe near the seat, grabbed the paddle, and splashed over the side. The boat tipped, then righted itself. I treaded water to warm up. Releasing the paddle, I watched it float away, then began a steady swim back to the shore. My face felt chilled, my breath loud to my ears, but my arms and legs loosened, and the shoreline drew steadily closer. My moose watched me from knee-deep in the pond, a mouthful of weeds hanging from his jaw.

When I reached the boat ramp, pale yellow and orange streaks lit the horizon, shadowing the trees into looming outlines, but the campground, thick with pines, remained dark. I saluted my moose, then tiptoed across the pine needles to the car where I retrieved my running shoes, windbreaker, and backpack; replaced the keys in the gas cap; pulled up my hood; and began my run along the empty backroads I'd learned so well over the year.

That night while I slept on the bus to California—my ticket bought with cash—Lauren notified campus security that I never returned with her car. As expected, they involved the local police, who found it parked at Lone Loon Pond—the canoe and paddle floating in the reeds. Not only was the lake too large to dredge, but the remains of the ghost town underneath thwarted any serious attempt at a search for my body. In the absence of a grieving family, there was no one to force the authorities to keep looking, no one to stand stricken on the lakeshore, no one for the local media to catch weeping in anguish. Upon digging deeper, it came out that not only was I a grieving orphan, but that I was pregnant, casting suspicion on whether it was an accident at all.

CHAPTER TWO

Lindsay

My mother always treated me as a bit of a science experiment. She wondered aloud what qualities I would develop, as if she had no control over the outcome. When I received good grades, she nodded as if something she had long suspected had been confirmed. When I proved to have athletic ability, she tipped her head and scrutinized me with a slight look of wonder, the way one would study modern art. When I told her I didn't believe in God despite her years of taking me to Sunday school, she recoiled as if she had no idea whose child I was.

People have always told me I look like my mother. We both have smooth dark hair, round faces, and dimples that people want to fit their fingers into. If it's the grocery store clerk or a waiter who points out our resemblance, we smile knowingly at each other. If it's someone we know better, my mother will say, "Isn't that funny since Lindsay's adopted."

Most times, they respond they never would've known. We smile knowingly at this too. Our similarities are in our mannerisms. I catch myself grabbing someone's arm to emphasize a point. Sticking my index finger up in the air when I have an idea. Worse is when I'm talking to someone and I hear her voice in my head improving their grammar. Or when I want to fix all the wrong abbreviations and autocorrects. It happens so often, I've resigned myself to it.

I never really asked about being adopted. It was just something I learned along with my numbers and the alphabet. My parents explained to me that I came out of my mother's heart instead of her stomach. This made perfect sense.

Once when I was home from college, as we pulled into the driveway in her Volvo, my mother mentioned that she'd been to the doctor that morning for a checkup.

"Is everything okay?" I asked.

"Well," she said, "I haven't gotten my period in a while and I wanted to make sure it was just menopause."

My mother's sagging white breasts pushed against my father's hairy beer belly flashed in my mind, and I felt that burning in the back of my throat from stomach acid coming up my esophagus.

"But I thought you couldn't have kids."

"Your father has a low sperm count." She glanced sideways at me. "So probably not, but you never know." She shrugged. "Thankfully, it's just menopause."

For the first time I imagined my parents as a young couple trying unsuccessfully to become pregnant and felt badly for them. Until I remembered I was not the first baby the adoption agency offered. According to my mother, they had had the option of a Latino boy, but they didn't feel equipped to raise him with proper cultural awareness so they passed. The next baby looked like a go until Stanford had a winning season and earned their spot in a bowl game. My mother promptly called the agency to say they had football tickets, so it really wasn't a good time to bring home a new baby. Imagine the stunned silence on the other end of the line. The agency questioning their decision to give my parents a child at all. One bowl-game victory later, my parents received a call that I was available. They accepted.

* * *

In their retirement, my parents are single-handedly keeping Beyond Borders in business. Under the tutelage of the educational tour company that caters to the lifelong-learner set, they've stomped their way through Chilean wineries studying traditional grape-growing techniques, frolicked with the iguanas on the Galapagos witnessing evolution in action, and ventured to Moscow and St. Petersburg to immerse themselves in classic Russian arts and literature. This month they are on a barge cruising down the Rhine.

When they travel, I am responsible for feeding the cat, watering the plants, and making sure their house is still standing when they return. The cat is getting up in years. Along with their itinerary, they always leave a note addressed to the vet giving me permission to make the ultimate judgment call. As if willing it to happen on my watch. Although they act as if the cat is an afterthought, I am always left instructions such as *Daniel will only eat if he is observed. Please stay until he is finished.* And *Turn the faucet to a light trickle. Daniel prefers drinking flowing water.*

Most of Daniel's teeth have been pulled in the last few years, so he has to gum down his food. Eating takes him twice as long as it would a cat with a full set of molars. As I sat at the kitchen counter watching him suck fish-shaped kibble, I flipped through their mail. My mother is on a first-name basis with her mailwoman, Dolores, and always leaves her a Christmas gift. Their mail comes in a sorted bundle carefully placed in their mailbox. Mine, a haphazard pile dumped on my front step. An L.L.Bean catalog caught my eye. When I reached for it the rest of the mail slid off the counter and scattered across the tiled floor. Daniel didn't even look up, causing me to suspect he was also going deaf.

Picking up the mail, I noticed a letter addressed to me. I expected to see Department of Motor Vehicles on the return—my parents lived in the house where I grew up and my driver's license still showed their street number—but it was from a law firm in Portland, Maine. Daniel still had half a bowl of food so I slid my finger under the flap. Inside was a note written in cryptic legalese that requested I contact Wilson & Cabot at my earliest convenience about my portion of the settlement of the estate of Claire Sullivan. My father had a cousin Claire somewhere on the East Coast, but I hardly knew her. Daniel continued to gum down his food, even though I wasn't watching.

"Thank you for calling so promptly," Robert Cabot said. Papers shuffled in the background. "Bear with me, Miss Williams. I have a few questions to ask. Can you confirm you were born on December 23, 1993 in Napa, California and your legal parents are Grace and Richard Williams?"

Daniel finally finished eating his food and leapt gracelessly into my lap, digging his claws in to avoid slipping. I plucked each claw from my skin as I verified my identity.

"One final question, Lindsay." He hesitated. "Were you adopted?"

I jerked to a stand. Daniel tumbled off my lap and landed on the tile with a thump.

"Who's Claire Sullivan?"

The Subzero refrigerator that blended with the cabinets hummed. The purified-water ice maker rumbled. Daniel stuck one foot in the air and began his postmeal tongue bath.

Robert Cabot cleared his throat. "Right. Claire Sullivan," he paused, "was your mother."

"My *birth* mother?"

"Yes."

"And she's dead?" I braced myself against the counter.

"Yes. She was in a car accident, blindsided. They said she never saw it coming."

I stared at one of the apples printed on the kitchen wallpaper, noticing the contrast of the shiny red body with the green stem. This same detail repeated in each apple.

"Thank you for telling me," I said, as if reading a Ms. Manner's script. "I appreciate the call."

"There's more," he said, before I could hang up. "Ms. Sullivan named you as her heir."

"Me?" I sank back onto a kitchen stool. "You understand I've never met her, right?"

His office chair squeaked. "I'd like to set up a meeting in my office. There's some paperwork that you'll need to sign before I can turn over the keys."

"Keys?"

"To the house here in Maine."

"I can't go to Maine," I said, raking my fingers through my hair. "I have to take care of Daniel."

"I'll send you a letter detailing the assets," he said. "The bulk of the estate is the property on Lone Loon Pond, plus she had stocks, mutual funds, and her life insurance policy."

"Doesn't she have anyone else to leave this to?"

"She named you in her will." He let this sink in a moment. "I'll send the letter today."

"Wait. Let me give you my address." I started pacing. "The address you have is my parents' house. I mean, the parents who raised me. I mean, my adoptive parents." I stopped and practiced my yoga breathing. "It's not where I actually live," I said.

"I understand."

"I'm glad one of us does."

★ ★ ★

Earthquakes give no warning. Sometimes animals act a little oddly in the preceding days, but people only put two and two together after the fact. Most native Californians store jugs of water, stockpile a week's worth of canned food, and live in houses bolted to their foundations. We don't hang decorative plates on our walls, affix heavy shelves over our beds, or place large statues on fireplace mantels. We know where to shut off our gas mains.

I checked the apple-shaped wall clock. It was the middle of the night in Germany. My parents only turned on their cell phone in emergencies, believing all news could wait until they returned. Especially news that might ruin a trip. I glanced around my mother's kitchen. Apple wallpaper. Apple dish towels. Tiny apples hanging from the chains attached to the ceiling fan to turn it on and off. I had even bought her an apple flowerpot one Mother's Day.

They'd upgraded the kitchen once they were through paying for my college. Installing radiant heat under the tile floor, a convection oven and a gas stove that gave the impression of people who actually cooked. The cookbooks on the counter were the same cookbooks that had been there all my life. If one were moved, there would probably be a darker spot behind it where the light never reached.

We'd eaten the same standard weekly dinners at the kitchen table every night except for Monday, when we ate in front of the football game thirty minutes behind kickoff so we could fast-forward through the commercials. Through the age of eighteen, I knew every quarterback, rusher, and wide receiver in the NFL but, starting in college, I rarely watched a game that wasn't the Super Bowl.

Next to the phone sat a homemade notepad made of scrap paper stapled together and a 2023 wall calendar from the Nature Conservancy with my mother's loopy handwriting escaping the confines of the boxes. *Tennis, church rummage sale,* and *book group* were scheduled for the week after they returned. I counted the days.

I started to text my best friend Emily, but wavered. Instead, as if needing an excuse, I snatched the watering can next to a bottle of Eleanor's Plant Food on the granite countertop and went straight to my father's study. I wet the soil of the ficus before setting the watering can on top of the file cabinet where it wouldn't leave a mark. Knowing my meticulous father, there would be a record. I pulled open drawers starting from the top. In the third drawer down, behind the half-drunk vodka bottle and alphabetized between *Acura Service* and *Board of Directors* was a file folder titled *Adoption*. I pulled it out and stared at it for a long moment. The manila folder had worn corners and stray ballpoint-pen marks on the front. I carried it to the desk and opened it.

On top sat the correspondence between the adoption agency and my parents that detailed the legal process of acquiring me. My satisfaction that they'd had to pay a fee mildly appalled me. Once when my cousin taunted me, I had retorted, "Oh yeah, my parents got to choose me, and yours just got stuck with you."

The papers had no reference to my natural parents, but they listed the name of the agency. Next were hospital records that gave my vital statistics at birth and the type of formula I was fed. And behind that several yellowed articles my mother—Grace—must have clipped out of Ann Landers's advice column. All with the same theme. Children who searched for their natural parents with grand dreams of who they would find and the utter disappointment when the truth was nowhere near as appealing as the fiction. I touched my fingertip to the family portrait my father had framed on his desk. My mother had prepared herself to support me before they even brought me home. This news could wait until after their trip.

Beneath the clippings was a letter typed in a script that was supposed to resemble handwriting. It was addressed to me, although it didn't have my name because she wouldn't have known it at the time.

My Daughter,

I know that there will be a time in your life when you are angry at the parents who are raising you. You will imagine a better life with me. You will question why I gave you up and what it was about you that made me not want you. Know that is not the case. I loved you and wanted you, but these wonderful people will be able to provide a better life for you. You are going to have to trust me, even though I have given you no reason to do so. You are the only person in the world to me, and this is why I made the hardest decision I hope ever to make. I know it was the right one, even if it may not feel that way to you at the moment. All I can do is assure you that you are loved. Loved by me. Loved by the parents whom you have grown up with, and that will never change no matter what happens.

Sincerely, Your Mother

Setting down the folder, I backed up a few steps until the cool wall stood firmly behind me. I pressed my hands to it behind my back. The file sat innocuously off-center on the blotter on my father's desk. In thirty years, the letter had never left that folder. I'd never acted out enough that my parents had needed to give it to me. I reached out and gently rubbed the corner of the letter between my thumb and forefinger as if touching fine fabric. Had I let Claire Sullivan down? After placing the contents back in their original order, I re-alphabetized the folder in the file cabinet and let the drawer close with a final, solid thud.

I walked down the hall, running my fingertips along the wallpaper as I once had done in the dark to find my bedroom entrance without waking my parents who slept with an open door. I hadn't touched the hall that way in years, but the light zipping sound of my fingertips on the slightly raised wall texture and the cool feel of the paper were as familiar to me as the scent of rosemary that drifted in my open bedroom windows during the summer. My bedroom no longer looked as it did when I lived here. Gone were the horse posters, pictures of my friends, stuffed animals, and clothes tossed across every surface. When I went to college, my mother had painted the room a pale pink, ordered matching flowered drapes, duvet cover, throw pillows, and an area rug that transformed the bedroom into a showroom. The room of the daughter she might have had.

"It looks like Laura Ashley puked in here," Emily had said.

I sank into the cradle of the pillows on the bed. The ceiling fan directed a light breeze over my body and cooled my flushed face. When the earth starts to rumble, Californians stand in the doorframe, move away from potential falling power lines, duck and cover under tables, and wait for the ground to stop shaking. Then we replace whatever has fallen off the shelves, sweep up the broken glass, make sure there are no new cracks in the foundation, and move on. I'd grown up on the San Andreas fault. Earthquakes were inevitable. We could only hope that when the Big One hit, we were prepared.

CHAPTER THREE

Claire

JOURNAL ENTRY, SEPTEMBER 1992

Let's go back to the beginning of the school year. Back to that night on Haskin's Hill. Back to when I was still innocent and trusting. Back to when I first met him. Picturesque Godfrey College perched on nine hundred acres overlooking the river and mill town below, which I had worked out to equal half an acre per student. Its symmetrical brick buildings trailed ivy, most of the student body played sports, and if the pictures were to be believed, the trees would flame into a postcard array of vibrant fall colors any minute.

A hand-drawn flier of a tent and campfire that claimed the Outing Club would provide "all the gear and beer" necessary for a campout caught my eye on the dorm's coed-bathroom door. After dinner, I grabbed a few extra layers and headed to Haskin's Hill. The night air had a slight damp chill, hinting at the long Maine winter to come. Following the sweet scent of wood smoke, I came upon a small tent village radiating out from a campfire where a group of students sucked keg beer and toasted marshmallows. I accepted a red plastic cup from a blond guy, knowing I wouldn't drink the vile liquid, and jammed two marshmallows onto a metal hanger. Most people seemed to know each other, and the conversation flowed around me about trips they'd taken and summer adventures. I stared into the flames, listened to their stories, and focused on my skewer, relieved at my return to anonymity.

"Those are the most perfectly toasted marshmallows I've ever seen," a voice said over my shoulder. He squatted beside me. "I don't have the patience. I just light mine on fire." He demonstrated, pulling a burning marshmallow from the flame, holding it to his lips like a smoking gun, and blowing it out. "I'm Will."

"Claire."

"Can I get you some graham crackers and chocolate to go with those perfectly toasted marshmallows?"

"Sure," I said.

He returned, offering a graham cracker layered with a square of Hershey's. The first bite reminded me of Girl Scout camping trips and campfires at the beach. Childhood times I'd blocked out.

"You're not a freshman, excuse me, 'first year,' " he made air quotes, "are you?"

"No, I'm a junior," I said. "Exchange student." I air-quoted back.

Will looked at me, waiting.

"From California. I thought I'd give this New England thing a try." I shrugged.

"Welcome to Maine, the way life should be."

I smirked. "And you?" Someone tuned a guitar in the shadows opposite the campfire.

"Senior." A whistle. "That's my cue. Excuse me." Will went and sat cross-legged next to the guitar player. I leaned back on my elbows and listened. These guys didn't hack their way through some classic rock ballad, nor were they screeching drunken karaoke. They sang in perfect sync, their voices blending in harmony.

Both dark-haired, athletic looking, and slightly preppy, Will wore a beat-up Godfrey baseball cap, jeans, and a fleece, while the guitar player wore a faded Exeter sweatshirt, wrinkled khakis, and striped wool socks. Will was attractive in that wholesome, boy-next-door kind of way and looked as if he should be working at the yacht club or carrying groceries for elderly ladies. The guitar player was dimpled and a little more rugged, like a mountaineer or sailor, but there was something dark, or maybe mischievous, behind his eyes that flashed a warning.

"They're good," I said to the closest girl.

She shrugged. "I heard that Trey took guitar lessons from like, Eric Clapton or Neil Young."

"Impressive."

"What else would they do with all that money? Godfrey doesn't need another field house."

"Right," I said. I watched them sing through the campfire, the flames casting flickering shadows on their features. My fingers were sticky from the marshmallows, and I pulled a sleeping bag around me for warmth. Eventually I snuck away from the fire, stretched out in the sleeping bag, soaked in the earthy smell of wet grass and decaying leaves, and stared into the starless black sky.

I woke to someone gently shaking me.

"Come on, it's raining. There's an empty tent over here."

I wiped rain from my face, gathered my damp gear, and followed him, spreading my sleeping bag in the tent and burrowing back into it. His body filled the doorway as he zipped the flap closed behind him, securing us inside. "That should keep the rain out." The tent smelled slightly musty, as if it hadn't quite dried before last being stuffed into its sack. "Man, you sleep like the dead."

I turned toward his voice, his features veiled by darkness. "Yeah, it can be a problem," I said. "And you are?"

"Apparently, your knight in shining armor." He laughed. "Trey."

I yawned. "Did you really take lessons from Clapton?"

"That's a new one." He snorted.

"Do people often make things up about you?"

"Are you a first year?"

"Junior. Exchange student."

"I wondered why I'd never seen you. I'd have remembered." The rain tapped a steady rhythm on the outside of the tent. "I was watching you watch us play. You have sad eyes." He moved closer. Wood smoke clung to his hair and his warm breath reached my lips.

I let the silence stretch. "You're dangerous," I said. I felt his kiss in the base of my spine, unlocking something long closed off, and then it was just the two of us in a damp tent, on a hill behind the dorms, in the middle of nine hundred acres, while the rain danced around us on the soft earth.

I woke alone, convinced I had dreamt the whole thing.

★ ★ ★

What you need to know, is one of the reasons I chose Godfrey was its lack of fraternities and sororities. It turned out the joke was on me. Even though the Greek system was abolished by unanimous vote five years before I arrived, rumors swirled about how women once refused to walk past the houses because of drunken assholes on the balconies holding up signs to rate them. There were stories of date-rape drugs, frostbite on bodies passed out in snowbanks, and something about defiling sheep. You had to petition to live off campus at Godfrey, and the administration was careful not to let the fraternities simply relocate down the hill. Despite this, Frat Row was still called Frat Row, even though the houses were now dorms named after prominent families in Maine.

To fill the gap, the sports teams took on the public role of social clubs, which is why Friday night my cross-country teammate, Lauren, and I went to a party hosted in the common room of an old frat house inhabited by several members of the football team. Lauren resembled a blond gazelle with flopping arms and legs and a ponytail that bounced out the back of her Godfrey baseball cap. She had freckles across her nose, a sly smile, and could talk as fluidly as she ran. During the first week of practice, we fell into a loping pace matching strides without trying, along Godfrey's wooded loop, and that ease continued off the running trails. A senior and captain of the team, Lauren was well-liked, well-known, and reveled in educating me on the ways of Godfrey.

The college might have cracked down on fraternities, but all you needed to have a keg in the dorm was the signature of someone over twenty-one on a party form and enough food and alternative beverages to counterbalance the volume of alcohol, the ratio conveniently detailed on said form. The football team possessed a supersized bag of stale tortilla chips that someone must have bought years before at a discount warehouse store and water with pink dye in plastic gallon milk jugs. Everyone knew not to eat the chips or drink the so-called punch.

Since the all-weather track circled the football field, Lauren and the rest of the team knew most of the players. As the night wore on, the keg flowed and several games of beer die raged in the corner by the tall windows. The more packed with drunken coeds the room became, the higher the temperature soared, so when someone started chanting "take it off, take it off" at one end of the room I didn't know what was happening until a bunch of naked, intoxicated "first years" tied together like a preppy chain gang shuffled down the grand staircase into the center of the party. Right behind them followed a conga line of clothed football players, the team captain bringing up the rear holding a boom box over his head belting "Eye of the Tiger."

"Really?" I said to Lauren. "The football team hazes? Tell me we don't do that for cross-country."

"It's not the football team, it's Alpha Tau."

"Can't you get expelled for that?"

She nodded.

"I don't understand. There shouldn't be any members left on campus."

"They went underground. They make their own rules now."

★ ★ ★

Lauren also educated me on the Royals. After one of our runs, I followed her across the marble floor of the cathedral-ceilinged dining hall to a table along the side. At the far end, a few dark wooden tables presided over the room from a raised section in front of floor-to-ceiling windows. "Good to see the Royals are in place," Lauren said, looking at the most prominent table.

"The Royals?" I glanced over my shoulder, setting my tray down and sitting.

"William Westin, Sloan Caldwell, and Theodore Charles Price III, otherwise known as Trey." She'd adopted a lock-jawed accent.

I nearly choked on my spaghetti. I thought Trey had evaporated with the rain.

"They run the school. They act friendly enough, but those three are a closed circuit. People say they're in some kind of satanic love triangle and they perform perverted sexual rituals on Haskin's Hill in the full moon, but all I know for sure is that Sloan and Trey have always been a couple. Why do you have that funny look on your face?"

"I met Trey and Will at the Outing Club campout."

"My advice?" She bit into a carrot stick. "Don't waste your time."

★ ★ ★

It was this exact advice I ignored when I stretched my calves against the metal bleachers the next day, spying. Sloan Caldwell was coltish with pale skin, large blue eyes, and dark hair tied back in a navy ribbon that matched her Godfrey field-hockey uniform. She'd rolled the top of her plaid skirt to shorten it to midthigh, and one of her socks drooped over her shin guard. She ran down the field brandishing her stick, protecting the ball from her opponent. She seemed to know where her teammates stood by instinct and controlled the game from center field. A small group of fans sat on the metal bleacher where I stretched. I heard my name and looked up. Will waved, gesturing to the empty seat next to him. Trey sat on his other side.

Climbing the metal bleachers, I arranged my face into a smile but felt my cheeks flush as I sank onto the cold bench next to Will. "Out for a run?" Will asked.

"Cross-country practice."

"Have you met Trey?"

Trey leaned forward and extended his hand. "You were at the Outing Club campout, right?"

"Right," I said. He held my hand a beat too long. I pulled away and stuffed my fists inside the front pocket of my hooded sweatshirt. "You two field-hockey fans?"

"Sloan gets all pissy if we don't show up." Will rolled his eyes. "She comes to our lacrosse games and thinks it's only fair we come to hers. Title IX and all that."

"Sloan?"

"Trey's girlfriend." Will pointed. "That midfielder who looks like she is going to club her opponent with her stick."

Trey's expression didn't change.

"Hey, are you coming to our show tonight?" Will asked. "It's in the CoHo. We can grab coffee after." Will elbowed Trey.

"Yeah, you should come," Trey said.

"Okay." I narrowed my eyes at Trey. "I better get going. Coach will be wondering what happened to me."

★ ★ ★

I arrived at the Coffee House alone and sank into the corner of one of the worn leather couches next to some upperclassmen I recognized from the football party. A good-sized crowd of students waited for the show to start, and I saw Sloan in a booth with some other girls. Steam condensed on the CoHo windows, and the rich scent of roasted beans wafted through the air. There was a small stage set on risers in the corner against a backdrop painted to look like the night skyline of a city, twinkling lights and all. The overhead lights dimmed and eight guys dressed in wrinkled khaki pants, button-down shirts rolled at the sleeve, and loosened ties took the stage. Trey stepped to the microphone. "Thank you all for coming. We're Looking for Treble." He winked, then pulled out a pitch pipe and blew a note.

"I'll give you some trouble," the broad-shouldered guy sitting on the other end of the couch said not quite under his breath to his L.L.Bean flannel-wearing buddy, who laughed.

The a cappella group sang a mix of current hits and barbershop classics. Trey and Will had most of the leads, their voices clear and strong, but their moves had to be self-choreographed. All eight hammed it up on stage, and the predominantly female audience responded as if this ragtag group rivaled the Beatles. "We love you, Trey," a gaggle of women shrieked from the back table. One glance at Sloan told me she was used to it.

"We need to take these guys down," Flannel whispered to Broad Shoulders. "The Royals, my ass. Let's get out of here." The football players snuck off, and two girls who had been sitting on the floor leaning against the couch arm slipped into their spots. They smiled at me.

A skinny soloist dedicated his song to his girlfriend,

crooning to her while she blew him kisses, but when Trey took the lead, he sang to the whole room. Will seemed to smile at the general audience, but when we caught eyes his face lit, and the girls next to me on the couch registered the attention with curiosity, one cupping her hand to whisper in her friend's ear. I'd always had a weakness for men who could sing, and Will's wholesome looks and affable charm on stage sparked my interest.

At the end of the show, Will came over. "What'd you think?"

"I loved it."

"Can you stay for coffee?"

"Sure." I smiled.

"You hold the couch and I'll order." Will walked up to the counter, and I watched people watch him. He seemed not to notice the attention, or maybe he was just used to it. I told myself it was because of his performance. Trey had slipped in next to Sloan and had his arm resting along the back of the booth, the girls she once sat with dispersed. Trey called to Will at the counter, inviting him over, but Will pointed at me.

"Hey, Claire," Trey called. "Come join us."

Will raised his shoulders in question, a coffee in each hand, and gave a sheepish smile. Sloan looked annoyed. I hesitated, then resigned myself to the inevitable and grabbed my coat to join them. Will let me slide in first, then scooted in, trapping me. I felt conspicuous, like everyone in the CoHo watched us from behind menus, around corners, and in the reflection off the windows, but none of the Royals seemed to notice.

"I saw part of your game today," I said to Sloan. "You're really good."

Her smile did not reach her eyes. "Thanks. Will says you're an exchange student." She sat back in the booth as if she had done her duty.

"Yep." I took a sip of my latte. "I always wondered what a small New England college would be like."

"And how do you like it?" Will asked.

"It's a whole different world," I said. He leaned toward me. "Everyone seems to know each other, and so many of you went to prep school, and then there's the tradition and the history. And let's not forget that it's going to snow."

"You've seen snow," Will said.

"Where I live, snow doesn't come to you, you go to it."

Sloan leaned her head on Trey's shoulder. "I've got an O'Chem test tomorrow. We should get going."

"Alright," Trey said. "Later, brother." He slapped Will's hand across the table. "Nice to see you, Claire."

I gave a limp half wave and watched them leave, feeling the extra sets of eyes exit with them, then snap back to us. I expected Will to move into the booth across from me, but instead he stretched his legs, placing his feet on the opposite bench, and slid his arm along the backrest behind me. It would have been easy to fit myself into the crook of his elbow, but instead I turned to face him and folded my leg underneath me, keeping a body-width of space between us. Will and I talked for another hour about safe topics. School, the sports teams we played on, our classes, his singing, and my love of reading, then he offered to walk me to my dorm room. Once there, he lingered in the doorway and I asked if he wanted to come in.

"I don't want to wake up your roommate," he said.

"I have a single."

"In that case." He glanced up and down the empty hall-way, then stepped inside. "Do you have a boyfriend back in California?" he asked.

"No. Why?"

"Because it seems like there's something you don't want to talk about."

"Not me, I'm an open book," I lied.

"I don't believe you." Will leaned over and kissed me, tasting like coffee. Even though I suspected I was being played, I didn't care. We ended up spending the night pressed together naked in my twin-sized bed. In the morning, I watched him sleep, his arm thrown up over his head and thought of Lauren's warning. Will woke, smiled, and pulled me closer. "I guess I'll be doing the walk of shame this morning," he said.

"I doubt it's your first time."

"Hey," he said, "it's not like I make a habit of this."

"No, you're part of a royal threesome."

Will sat on the side of the bed and pulled on his t-shirt. "Yeah, and on the full moon we make sacrifices to the Pagan gods."

"You do, don't you?"

"We all have our secrets," he said.

CHAPTER FOUR

Claire

JOURNAL ENTRY, OCTOBER 1992

Maybe it was my own aloofness, or that I was from away, or because we were all so adept at avoiding talking about our families, but the Royals slowly let me in without any special effort on my part. "You seem to have gotten awfully chummy with Will," Lauren said on one of our long runs down a stretch of maple-lined lane, the leaves flaming their vibrant autumn hues as promised in the brochure. "Be careful. They're not who they appear to be."

She told me the boys' fathers were Delta Kappa Epsilon members at Godfrey and that Trey's father, Theodore Charles Price II, aka Chaz, once fraternity president and then president of the advisory board, was loudest in his opposition to abolishing the fraternities. He threatened to withdraw his financial support, but in the end tradition won. All Price men had attended Godfrey, and Trey would be no exception. "I went to Exeter with them and my father knows Chaz from business. He says he can go from Dr. Jekyll to Mr. Hyde in the time it takes you to disagree with him. You can bet that DKE is alive and well, and Will and Trey are behind it."

★ ★ ★

On a random Thursday, I sat eating lunch alone in the dining hall, rereading Flannery O'Connor before my Best American Short Story class, when Sloan plunked herself down across from me at the small table. "I think I just failed my history test."

I looked up, startled. Sloan was one of those women who always appeared to have just rolled out of bed after sex. A sensuality wafted off of her whether she was with Trey, a girlfriend, or a professor and, even when I saw her walking or talking with someone at a distance, it felt like spying on something illicit. Sloan and I had never eaten a meal alone, but she had defrosted over the last month.

"Where are Will and Trey?" I asked.

"At a meeting."

"Sorry about the test," I said.

She picked up her fork and held it poised over her salad. "So, you and Will, huh?"

"I guess." No one dated in the traditional sense at Godfrey, mainly because there wasn't anywhere to go on a date. Instead you were either hooking up when drunk or in a serious relationship. Will and I had been hanging out, studying together, eating lunch when our class schedule aligned, going for runs around the campus loop, and having regular sex, but we kept an emotional arm's length. It was the perfect arrangement for me. Attraction, companionship, and no expectations to be the person I was before losing my parents.

"Will's a good guy," she said. "He needs someone he can trust."

I studied her face. As with all my conversations with the Royals, it was what wasn't being said that was the most interesting. "When did you and Trey start dating?"

"From the womb."

"Didn't you ever want to be with someone else?" I took a bite of my sandwich.

"We've had our rough patches." She stabbed a cucumber

slice from her salad with her fork. "But everyone knows we'll end up together so, if that means I need to look the other way sometimes, I do."

"But you want to be together."

"It's expected."

"That's not the same thing."

"It is," she said.

★ ★ ★

The following week, I hid myself in a leather chair deep in the labyrinth of the library and studied for my midterms by the halo of a reading lamp. Two of the things I loved most about the library were the towers of old books crammed every which way in a building that had long ago run out of shelf space and the study spots tucked into forgotten corners for people like me who never aged out of needing a secret hideout. The main lights in this section operated on a timer that I never bothered to twist, and I had yet to see anyone else back here. The library closed at midnight, but no one checked the dark corners, so I often ended up locked in when I studied late.

It was somewhere around 2:00 a.m. when I packed my bags and clicked off my reading lamp, throwing myself into darkness, when I caught a slinking shape out of the corner of my eye. I tensed, stilled my breath, and pressed myself to the end of the stack, blending into the shadows. The figure seemed to know where they were going. His profile, familiar.

"Trey?" He whipped around toward my voice and froze. "Is that you? It's Claire." I stepped into his sight.

He relaxed. "Claire? What are you doing here?"

"I could ask you the same thing."

"Are you alone?"

"I thought I was."

"Come on." He took my hand and I became hyperconscious

of the dry warmth of his fingers laced through mine. He led me around a few more turns to an unobtrusive door, where he cocked his head, raised his eyebrows, gave me a wicked smile, then twisted the knob, and pulled me through, nudging the door shut behind us. We stood in a bare-planked room with an old wooden circular staircase ascending through the middle. Moonlight poured down from windows, and the temperature in the uninsulated space plummeted twenty degrees from the warmth of the library.

"After you," Trey gestured to the stairway.

I took hold of the rough banister and climbed the rickety steps until I reached a wooden platform encircled by windows. Trey pushed open a pane and crawled out. I followed. We stood on a protected widow's walk on the outside of the library clock tower, which housed the glowing beacon of light that shone over campus.

"This is the highest point on Godfrey Hill," Trey said. Streetlights illuminated the neighborhoods of Babcock Falls below us. Most of the households were dark with sleep. Steam billowed from the paper-mill stack and floated across the sky like its own milky way. In the distance, the moon reflected off the dark surface of a lake like a double spotlight.

"Gorgeous." The clear night sky shimmered with endless stars. I zipped my jacket and wrapped my arms around myself, stuffing my hands into my armpits. "Wow, it's freezing. If this is October, how's it going to be in January?"

Trey stepped behind me and wrapped his arms around my body, his warmth penetrating my layers. He pressed his rough, stubbled cheek to mine.

"Do you know the legend of the clocktower light?" I shook my head. "It's rumored that if a virgin ever graduates from Godfrey it will go out." His breath caressed my neck and he tightened his hold. I relaxed back into his body. His warm hands slid under my layers to press against my bare skin. The tent had not been a dream after all.

I never asked his reason for sneaking around the library during the witching hour.

★ ★ ★

Godfrey's chapel, built on the top of a grassy hill surrounded by blazing trees, may as well have stood in Salem's town square during the witch trials. The chapel screamed classic New England Puritan design. Red brick, white trim, wrought-iron railings that coaxed visitors to the oversized front door, and a carillon bell tower pointing into the heavens. Tonight, Halloween—when fog poured down the candlelit steps to the cobweb-covered door, and shrieks of witches echoed from inside—marked my first visit to its hallowed walls. Slightly unsettled by the bone-chilling cries, I followed the Royals inside the dimly lit chapel. The only illumination emanated from flickering pillar candles, a single gothic chandelier, and the ghoulish jack-o-lanterns lining the aisles. The tall, narrow building had parallel arched balconies running its length, which housed seating that overlooked the red velvet pews in the nave below. Students packed every spot and we squeezed into the last row of the balcony, our arrival marked by the usual ripple. A hooded figure hunched over the immense pipe organ in the apse played macabre music suitable to Dracula's castle. When the chapel doors slammed shut with an echoing boom, I jumped. Will grabbed my hand and squeezed.

The last strains of organ music faded and the chapel fell dead silent, as if everyone feared to even breathe. A figure in a floor-length black robe floated down the foggy aisle holding a candle to light his path to the pulpit. When he threw off his hood to reveal deliberately wild grey hair and wire-rimmed glasses, I expected an accompanying bolt of lightning and crash of thunder. Pushing his glasses higher on his nose, Professor Boone made a production of opening a large, weathered book and then began to read. *In the bosom of one of those spacious coves which indent the eastern shore of the Hudson* . . .

The four of us filled the back pew, Sloan and I sandwiched by the boys. We had shed our outer layers, but I still wore my hat and scarf to ward off an imagined chill. The Halloween ghost stories were a highlight of Godfrey's academic year. Every rapt face turned toward the pulpit, their shadowy features lit by the soft yellow of flickering candles. When Professor Boone turned the last page of "The Legend of Sleepy Hollow," the specter at the organ resumed his haunting theme, and a second hooded reader floated down the jack-o-lantern aisle, revealing herself as a makeup-wizened Professor Woodrow. She began reading from her cobwebbed book. *Without, the night was cold and wet, but in the small parlour of Laburnam Villa the blinds were drawn and the fire burned brightly.*

Trey and I had not spoken since the library tower, as if staying silent kept our actions from being real. Both boys had been mysteriously absent for most of the last two weeks, disappearing at odd times and sharing meaningful glances when they thought they were unobserved. Rumors circulated that Alpha Tau members' rooms had been broken into, their toothbrushes stolen, used to scrub in various horrifying places, and returned to the unsuspecting owners who continued to use them until revealing photographs were slipped under the doors a week later.

The hairs on the back of my neck rose as Professor Woodrow read the part of "The Monkey's Paw" where the old man has made the second wish as his desperate wife is running to the front door to let in their dead son. Behind us a door creaked on its hinges, and a soft footfall pattered on the wooden balcony floor. The air tightened and I whipped my head around. Nothing but empty darkness. I glanced at Will focused on Professor Boone reading "The Tell-Tale Heart" in a creepy voice.

"Did you hear that?" I whispered.

"It's the heart," Will said.

"I'm not kidding. Something is wrong. I can feel it."

"You're cute when you're scared." He kissed my nose and turned his attention back to the story.

The shadow of a figure loomed life-sized in the archway, then disappeared. I touched Sloan with light fingers on her knee.

"We're being watched."

"We're always being watched," she said.

I took a deep, stilling breath.

Professor Boone read the last line, *I admit the deed!—tear up the planks! here, here!—It is the beating of his hideous heart!* and as the eerie music crescendoed through the chapel, swift movement stirred the air behind us in the darkness.

A rough hand clamped over my mouth, muffling my scream. I jabbed my elbow into whoever was holding me and tried to pry his hand off my face. Shadowy ski-masked figures grabbed Will. I took hold of his arm, but they dragged him and Trey out through a flush balcony door, their struggles muffled by the pipe organ. Once released, Sloan and I stared at each other, wide-eyed, alone on the pew next to Will and Trey's abandoned coats and gloves.

★ ★ ★

Back in Sloan's room, she paced in front of me as I perched on her flowered bedspread, trying not to think about what she and Trey did in that bed.

"They'll call," she said.

"How can you be so sure?"

"This has got to be that stupid fraternity shit."

"What fraternity shit?"

"Oh please, Claire. Don't pretend."

"Do you think they're okay?"

"I hope so," she sighed. "As soon as they can get to a phone, they'll call," she said. We both stared at the off-white receiver sitting idle in its cradle.

"You're sure there's no message tone?" I asked

"Yes," she said. "Be my guest. Pick it up yourself."

As soon as I hung the phone back up, it rang. Sloan snatched the handset.

"Yes, I'll accept the charges," she said. "Thank God. We'll be right there—" She paused. "What do you mean who? Me and Claire. Yes." She hung up. "They're fine. Pissed off, but fine. Bring their jackets. We need to stop by their room and get clothes."

We pulled into the campground parking lot at Lone Loon Pond in Sloan's green Saab with the ubiquitous *Green Mountain Coffee* and *Mad River Glen Ski It If You Can* bumper stickers. They waited for us on the picnic table, Trey wrapped in a blue tarp that looked like it belonged over a woodpile and Will wearing a black Hefty garbage bag. Anger radiated from their bodies and I stood back silently while they yanked on their clothes, then piled into the car.

"Crank the heat," Trey said.

"Are you okay?" I asked.

"We're fine," Trey said through clenched teeth.

"What happened?" Sloan asked. Trey glared at her profile and then glanced into the back seat at Will sitting next to me. "Come on," Sloan said.

"Just tell them," Will said.

Trey shook his head and stared out the window at the woods rushing by.

"You know you can trust me to keep my mouth shut," I said.

Trey acted like he hadn't heard me.

"Fine, I'll tell them," Will said. They'd been dragged down the chapel's back staircase with pillowcases over their heads, loaded into a waiting car, and driven out to the middle of the woods where they were stripped and left. "We didn't see any faces," Will said. "But as they drove away they called, 'The Royals have no robes.' Hysterical, huh?"

They had walked toward lights until they saw a house and figured out they were on Lone Loon Pond. They knew about the campground payphone from their Outing Club trips.

"They're going to pay for this," Trey said.

In the morning, fliers hung all over campus with a picture of them naked and the caption, *The Royals Disrobed*. I saved one before they were torn down.

CHAPTER FIVE

Lindsay

Fieldstone walls and maple trees lined the long, winding driveway. I checked the paper in the passenger seat one more time for confirmation. The numbers still matched. A grey farmhouse with a large wraparound front porch bearing two Adirondack chairs waited at the end of the driveway. Clumps of bright orange tiger lilies clustered along the side of the house. Despite being only a few hours away when I lived in Boston after college, my only experience with Maine was going to L.L.Bean at four o'clock in the morning because they claimed to be open twenty-four hours a day, three hundred and sixty-five days a year, and when you are young and have been cooped up all winter, going to see if this was true sounded like fun. When the attorney had said a house in Maine, I had pictured a little log cabin perched on the edge of a still blue pond, surrounded by dense woodlands.

I parked the car in front of the porch and sat for a moment listening to the engine tick as it cooled. I mentally added *wraparound porch* to my list of ideal-house features. A large beech tree with a trunk that I couldn't stretch my arms all the way around shaded the front yard. The side yard housed a gated garden with rows of raised planting beds. *Garden* went on the list too. In California, the fence would keep out deer, but I wasn't sure what critters found vegetables to be fine dining in Maine. Moose? Whatever plants once thrived were now losing the battle to a tangle of wildflowers and weeds. Claire Sullivan must have been a gardener.

I exited the car, took three steps up onto the solid wooden porch of the farmhouse, and turned to look down the driveway—my driveway. The road was visible, but another car hadn't come by in the ten minutes since I'd arrived. The papers stated the lot was almost five acres. The term "lot" was a misnomer. California had lots surrounded by six-foot fences. This was more like a farm. It reminded me of the place in the foothills of the Santa Cruz Mountains I frequented as a child, once owned by a family who used it as a working farm, then donated it to the local open-space district. The nonprofit that maintained the property planted an organic vegetable garden the size of a football field, operated a CSA, kept goats, sheep, and chickens for kids to pet, and hosted a number of horse shows each summer where I cantered my swaybacked mare around the two-foot jump courses for ribbons. It wasn't the kind of show the kids from the pony club attended, and that made it perfect. When the nonprofit wasn't hosting an event, I rode my horse along the trails, jumping over fallen oak branches and connecting to miles of paths that would take me to the ocean if I dared.

Reaching my hand into my pocket, I pulled out the key Robert Cabot had given me and fit it into the lock. It turned easily and the door swung inward. I hesitated before stepping across the threshold and centered myself on my breathing like at the start of my yoga class.

Inside the farmhouse, the air had a stillness about it and smelled stale. A navy pea coat and dog leash hung on a coat rack inside the door. A pair of garden clogs were tucked neatly under a wooden bench. Next to the bench sat a basket containing a few chewed tennis balls, a stuffed hedgehog, and a bone. This house was not staged for sale. This was how Claire Sullivan lived.

I moved down the entry hall like a timid fangirl given access to her most revered celebrity's home. The hall ended in an open, high-ceilinged living room with a prominent stone fireplace and bookshelf-lined walls. Prayer flags strung artfully along the far wall. Old wooden snow shoes crossed over the mantle. A dog bed lay at the base of the fireplace. Framed pictures taunted from the bookshelves. I stared but did not pick them up. The same woman repeated in multiple photos with different smiling strangers. I searched her features. She had dark hair, high cheekbones, and an impish look in her eye, as if she were up to something only she knew about.

I ran my finger along the book spines, *Peterson Field Guide to Birds, AMC Guide to The Appalachian Trail, Cross-Country Ski Trails of New England,* and *The Cook's Garden.* The next shelf housed *Jane Eyre, To Kill a Mockingbird, A Separate Peace,* and then a prickle at the back of my neck—the complete works of Jane Austen, my mother's favorites. My mother had read to me every night as a child. Even when I was well past being able to read on my own. She liked the classics, *The Five Little Peppers and How They Grew, Rebecca of Sunnybrook Farm, Anne of Green Gables.* I remembered begging her to please stop crying and finish reading me *Charlotte's Web.*

I escaped into the kitchen.

A rack of immaculate copper-bottomed pots hung over the center island. The granite counters boasted a turquoise Kitchen Aid mixer, a shiny combination coffee/espresso press, and a wooden block with professional-grade knives. Unlike my parents' showroom kitchen, this one felt well-used. The Viking gas range was large enough to cook for a full restaurant. Hand-labeled spice jars crowded together on the counter within easy reach. Affixed to the front of the French-doored refrigerator was a Gary Larson cartoon with a dog, paws clasped together thinking "oh please, oh please" while trying to lure a cat into an open dryer with the words "cat fud" and an arrow. Several pictures of a black lab. A postcard from the Galapagos Islands. And the Robert Frost quote about the two paths.

Crossing back through the living room, I glanced into the office where a large antique white desk with a computer filled the room. I flashed to searching through his files in my father's den and backed out. I ran my hand along the smooth wood of the banister, picturing her long, graceful fingers, then remembered the garden and revised them to be a little rougher with dirt under the nails.

I made my way upstairs. Off the hallway sat Jack-and-Jill guest rooms split by a bathroom. I pushed open the main bedroom door, then hesitated. Centered in the room was a tidily made sleigh bed flanked by two coffee-toned nightstands. Opposite stood a dresser and a fireplace with neatly stacked wood on the hearth, ready for a winter night. *Fireplace in bedroom* was added and checked off the list. The smooth comforter, the precision of the throw pillows, and the lack of clutter on the dresser all yelled staged, until I saw the haphazard stack of books and magazines on the nightstand. I ran a finger along the mantle, careful not to touch the pictures. More of her arm-in-arm with friends and one with her holding a walking stick with her dog by her side, a stick in his mouth. I wondered who had adopted the dog.

The attached bathroom hid a jet tub that did not match the early Colonial design, with half-melted candles of all colors, shapes, and sizes clustered around the edges, and a large bottle of vanilla bubble bath. The hand soap and lotion next to the sink claimed to be for "the pampered gardener." I squirted some on my hand and inhaled the scent of lavender and lemons. This must be

what she smelled like. My mother always smelled of Oil of Olay.
I opened the medicine cabinet to ibuprofen, hydrogen peroxide,
and Band-Aids.

I stared at my reflection in the mirror. Using my fingers, I
stretched and massaged my features like someone practicing funny
faces. Where my mother Grace and I had the same dimples, Claire
and I had the same cheekbones and translucent skin. Where my
mother had full, thick hair a shade darker than mine, Claire had
what looked to be the same finespun hair that I struggled to make
look fuller. It was hard to be objective. My face and my mother's
were each as familiar to me as the other. Claire's face, new.

Back in the bedroom, I walked over to the dresser and opened
the jewelry box. I didn't see it at first, but then the distinct blue
color caught my eye. I lifted out a bracelet from my collection.
It was one of my favorite designs. Hand-blown glass beads in a
deep azure alternating with sea glass, connected with a delicate
silver thread meant to look like a web covered in dew. It didn't
stop there. She had several other pieces. Mainly necklaces and
bracelets. All of them handmade by me. My throat went dry.
Tears threatened. I backed up until I sat on the edge of the bed. I
didn't sell my jewelry in any local shops.

I was fingering the azure bracelet again, when a voice called
from downstairs, startling me. Fastening it on my wrist, I yelled,
"Coming," and scrambled from the room. I swung around the
knob of the banister, feeling the smooth wood against my palm,
and stopped just short of knocking into a woman standing in
the entryway beaming at me. She had cropped grey hair, piercing blue eyes, and wore a navy tank top, khaki Bermuda shorts,
and orange Crocs. She looked to be in her midfifties, her age in
the crow's feet at the corners of her eyes and laugh lines around
her mouth.

"You must be Lindsay," she said. She clasped her hands
together and then reached out for mine. She held my arms away

from me as my grandmother often did to get a better look at me. "You're the spitting image of Claire," she said. "It's almost like having her back." She squeezed my hands.

"I look like her?"

"Look at those cheekbones." She clasped my face between her hands and a sad look came over her. "Losing her was awful." I swallowed hard.

"Oh goodness, gracious me," she said. "I just barged in here and didn't introduce myself. I'm Beverly, Claire's neighbor and best friend for the last ten years." She stuck out her hand. I shook it.

"Are you the one who's been watching the house?"

"Yes, that's me. Riley's with Lucas. Another friend. He'll bring him over whenever you're ready."

"Riley?"

"Claire's dog, well, I guess your dog now. What's wrong, dear?"

I clung to the banister. "Sorry, it's just that no one said anything about a dog."

"It's okay, honey. I'll help you sort it out. Claire would've done anything for me and I for her. You're her daughter, which makes you my family now. I've been watering the houseplants, but I'm afraid I've let the garden go. It's a shame really. Claire loved that garden. I usually found her bent over one of the beds weeding or trimming lettuce when I came over for coffee. She liked to spend as much time as possible outside. We'd pull the chairs up and just sit for hours." Her voice drifted off. "But listen to me, I'm going on and on."

"No, it's nice," I said. "I don't know anything about her."

"We'll have to fix that." She patted my arm. "I just wanted to pop in and introduce myself. I live in the next house over." Beverly ushered me outside. "You can just see the corner of the porch if you look over there through the trees. You'll see it much clearer in the winter." She gave my elbow one more squeeze and bounced down the steps, her arms swinging with her stride, and the word winter hanging in the air like a snowflake.

★ ★ ★

After breaking up with Chris, the boyfriend everyone assumed I would marry, I had searched for my own place to buy before the skyrocketing prices edged me out of the market. I hoped my savings, coupled with my steady position as a private art-gallery manager and my growing jewelry business, would be enough. Eileen, my mother's friend and my realtor, had challenged me to write a description of my ideal house.

"If you know what you want, you'll find it," she said, sounding more Zen master than real-estate agent. "This is hard for some people." It took me only a few minutes. *Lots of light. High ceilings. A fireplace. Enough space to host eight for dinner. A place for all my books and somewhere cozy to read. A jewelry studio!! A fenced-in yard with room for a barbecue, table, and chairs* and seeing as this is a fantasy world, let's add a *hot tub. A garage for a few bikes, camping gear,* and *skis.* I put the cap on my pen and then took it off again. *Easy parking.* I underlined it three times.

On our first day looking, Eileen picked me up in her Lexus. "College Terrace is an acquired taste," she said standing in front of my rented Palo Alto house in her matching pumps, purse, and one of my bracelets—a delicate sapphire and leaf design—dangling from her wrist. My mother's friends were some of my best customers. As I often reminded myself when they made me crazy.

I looked up and down the street. The houses were an odd mix of fixed-up old adobe cottages and looming modern houses that stretched across as much of the lot as possible while still leaving the mandatory strip of landscape between the exterior wall and the six-foot fence that enclosed the yards. Mature trees lined the street. I knew the names of all my neighbors. And I left my front door unlocked without worrying during the rainy season, when the wood swelled and it wouldn't shut all the way. Even the weekly Wednesday-night parade of critical-mass rollerbladers and the enterprising little girl across the street who set up a lemonade stand for a dollar a glass held a certain charm for me. So what if I'd referred to the house I lived in for the last five years as the Southwestern Jail and routinely gave directions stating mine was the third adobe shoebox in the row, the one without the decorative bars. The neighborhood was a great mix of new young families drawn by the top school district, Stanford grad students, and people who had lived there since a home cost fifty thousand dollars instead of the current million-plus asking price. And I could afford the rent.

Eileen piloted the car to the older section of town where the university professors, the dot-com millionaires, and she lived. Her goal was to show me the difference between a $700,000, $800,000, and $1,000,000 home. I surfed waves with my hand out the car window and embraced the insanity. The first couple homes, I wouldn't even rent. They had crooked walls, sagging ceilings, rusted fixtures, and warped, outdated linoleum that peeled up at the corners.

"You've got to be kidding," I said.

Eileen just shook her head solemnly. "I knew you had to see it for yourself. Why don't I drive you around some of the other neighborhoods?" She handed me a map while shifting into drive. "The great thing is each neighborhood pocket has its own feel." We turned down a twisted, tree-lined street without sidewalks.

"This is nice," I said.

"If you don't mind hearing the Mariachi bands in the park on Sunday."

I bit my tongue and decided to just look out the window at all the houses whizzing by, pretending it was as simple as picking the one I wanted.

"How about we look at the next price level up?" Eileen said. At least now we were into the range of houses that I would rent. Each house we walked into was professionally staged with cozy furniture, shiny fruit bowls, and fake photographs of smiling, happy families. Eileen would immediately start talking about Feng Shui, blocked chi, which walls could be removed, where windows could be added, and the best way to fit a Jacuzzi tub into a substandard bathroom. I walked around thinking that I could make do with a small kitchen since I didn't cook well. If there was no closet space, I could give away the clothes I didn't wear enough. Or that I didn't really need a garage that would fit my car. Just my toys.

The house I grew up in was old by California standards. Built after the great 1906 earthquake and modeled on the House of the Future at the World's Fair. It was the summer home of a family who lived in San Francisco. When the journey to what was then the Santa Clara Valley—before silicon and the computer industry—constituted a half-day affair in a carriage. I'd exasperated Eileen until she took me to a house she referred to as "dilapidated," en route to the next cookie-cutter listing.

"Now this is one I could actually picture myself in," I'd said.

She'd smiled slowly. "You grew up in a unique house," she said more to herself than to me. "That's shaped your idea of home." Eileen was not one to turn down a challenge. The next round of houses we looked at had character.

★ ★ ★

A thunderstorm rolled through in the middle of the night in Maine. I made a fire and watched the shadows creep across the walls from my makeshift bed on the couch. My parents slept unaware in their floating stateroom on a barge somewhere in Germany. The house creaked. My friends all believed my eccentric childhood home was haunted (which I capitalized on at Halloween, insisting on a party and a Haunted House), but the only ghosts were those of the imagination. Now, deep under the comforter listening to the familiar groans of an old house and watching the colors of the flame devour the log, I finally began to relax.

Rain pattered on the roof and soothed me to sleep like a slow massage. The weather in Northern California is dependable— warm and sunny in the spring, summer, and fall and then it starts to rain. Some years it rains so hard that the earth can't absorb the water as quickly as it falls, and that is when roads flood, backyards become lakes, and multimillion-dollar homes slide down mud slopes to their demise.

CHAPTER SIX

Lindsay

After two false starts, I figured out how to use the shiny, high-tech coffee maker and was lounging in one of the Adirondack chairs sipping a latte listening to the *New Yorker Fiction* podcast, when a mud-splattered pickup truck turned down the driveway. A black dog bounced in the bed, pulling excitedly on his short tether. The truck door opened and a guy wearing jeans, a t-shirt, and a baseball cap waved to me as he slid off the seat. He fiddled at the dog's neck for a minute, then eighty pounds of Labrador retriever leapt over the side of the truck and tore up the driveway. The guy followed at a more normal pace with the easy gait of an athlete.

When the dog reached me, he licked my coffee cup and pawed at the door with both ears cocked. I turned the knob. He rushed past me, dove into the toy basket, rummaged around with his nose, and emerged with a tennis ball that he dropped at my feet. When I stepped back outside to throw it, I came face-to-face with the pickup-truck driver standing on the porch.

"I see you've already met Riley," he said extending his hand. "I'm Lucas."

"Lindsay," I said, switching the slobber-covered ball to my other hand and wiping my fingers on my jeans. The dog's eyes followed the ball. I threw it as hard as I could down the drive-way. He chased after it with a practiced leap off the porch.

"He's not always this crazy," Lucas said, nodding at the dog. "I think he's just excited to be home. I would've called before coming, but I think the phone has been shut off, or the lines are down due to the storm."

"Oh, right. Well, thanks for taking care of him. I'm sure Claire would have appreciated it." I'd been saying her name in my head, but it was the first time I'd said it out loud. My lips didn't quite form around it.

"Not a problem, she meant a lot to my mom."

I looked at him a little more closely. He was younger than I'd thought, with broad shoulders, slim hips, and dark hair curling out from under his baseball hat.

"You knew her well?"

"Yeah, she was my mother's best friend. I've known her since I was little. She was part of our family." His eyes went to the ground and his voice trailed off.

"Latte?" I asked. "I think I've mastered the machine." The dog returned and dropped the ball at my feet.

"He never gets tired of that ball. Eventually you have to hide it." Lucas scratched him behind the ears and the dog leaned into him. "I'm going to miss the guy."

"Whoa," I erased his sentence from the air with my hands. "I'm just here for a short visit. If you could keep him longer, that would be great."

"You're not staying?"

"Um, no. I mean, I hadn't planned to." I fidgeted with the hem of my t-shirt. "I hadn't even planned to come to the house. I just went to sign the papers, and then the lawyer gave me the key so I came here and . . ." my voice drifted off and it was my turn to study my shoes.

"A latte sounds great," he said.

I returned to find Lucas relaxed in an Adirondack chair and the dog sprawled at his feet chewing the tennis ball. I handed Lucas the cup and sat next to him.

"Quite a storm last night," he said. We sat and sipped our coffees. *Attractive male neighbor*, I added to my list. Check.

★ ★ ★

When Lucas heard I hadn't made my way to the pond yet, he insisted on going home to retrieve his canoe. The dog stopped chewing his ball to watch Lucas walk down the driveway, then looked at me.

"Shall we check out the pond?" I said to the dog. He led me down the porch steps and along the curved pathway Lucas had pointed out, pausing at a thick band of trees cut by a trail. At the end, a small dock jutted into the water.

Pond was a misnomer. It wasn't a lily-pad-covered, dank body of water filled with frogs, insects, and a bottom squishy with dead plant matter that would ooze unpleasantly between your toes. Not to mention leeches. This was a lake. The shoreline twisted and curved, reaching its fingers into the trees like the fog that crept inland at home. The other shore was visible, but I wouldn't dare swim it. A loon called from across the water, sounding eerily like a woman in distress. Another answered somewhere off in the bushes.

The dog appeared at my side holding a large stick and then ran to the end of the dock. He looked over his shoulder at me, as if to ask what I was waiting for. I flung the stick like a boomerang into the water. The dog did a tuck dive off the end of the dock and swam in an efficient paddle to the stick, his tail wagging like a rudder. He exited on the shore, trotted back, and dropped the stick on my sneaker before shaking off his coat and staring at the water again, ready to pounce. By the time Lucas found us, we were both soaked.

We lowered the canoe into the water, and Lucas held the stern while I climbed into the bow. The dog jumped into the middle and distributed his weight along the bottom.

"He looks like an old pro," I said.

"It took a while for him to settle, but I like the company when I'm fishing," Lucas said. "Riley still gets excited when he sees a merganser, but he's learned not to lunge at them."

We paddled smoothly away from the dock. It hadn't escaped me how easily Lucas lifted the canoe out of the back of his truck by himself, the muscles in his arms flexing through his t-shirt, or that he assumed I could carry my end. Lucas had a gentleman's courtesy. Saying please and thank you, and letting me walk ahead of him. He had changed into a pair of Keens and khaki shorts that showed off his long, strong legs. Evenly tanned and sexy.

We paddled parallel to the shore. Lucas worked for a consulting firm completing environmental-impact reports and recreational surveys for whatever entity hired them. His clients ranged from the paper mills—some of the largest forestland owners in Maine—to the Nature Conservancy, to the power companies who needed to time their dam releases with the height of the river-rafting season.

"So let me get this straight," I said. "They pay you to go river rafting?"

"Someone has to test the water level." He winked. "But one of the hazards of the job is you never look at the natural world the same way again. You're either calculating the volume of visitors a park can have without negatively impacting the trails, or you're identifying all the plants and trees in sight, or you're looking over the side of your canoe for water clarity and don't realize you're doing it until you're reaching for your notepad. Sometimes I miss just enjoying nature."

I looked over the bow of the canoe into the velvet-blue water. The shadowy figures of fallen trees reached up to me from the murky depths. The bleached branches looked like ghostly arms trying to wrap me into a watery embrace. I shivered.

"I don't know which is worse," I said. "Being able to see clearly under the surface, or being blissfully unaware of what's lurking." I pushed the sleeves of my shirt up to my elbows and stabbed the paddle back into the water.

"Cool bracelet," he said. "It looks like something Claire would wear."

I looked down at my exposed wrist. I still wore the piece I'd found in her jewelry box.

"It's one of my designs," I said.

"Your designs?"

"I design jewelry. It was just a hobby, but it took on a life of its own and now it's my side gig. My main job is managing a private art collection for a very wealthy Silicon Valley family."

"It makes sense you and Claire would have the same taste," he said.

My shoulders twitched and I mis-stroked, banging the paddle against the side of the canoe. The dog's head popped up. He glanced around, then returned to resting his chin on his front paws. I hoped he was the only one who registered my discomfort.

"Let's explore over there." I pointed to one of the coves with my paddle.

Lucas nodded. "There's some pretty yellow birch hidden around the corner." We matched strokes. Lucas navigated us around the point and into the hidden finger. A few docks extended from the shore and an occasional house appeared through the trees, but the pond felt like our own private treasure.

"It's beautiful here," I said. I set my paddle in the bottom of the boat, leaned forward, and spread my fingers in the cold water on either side of the pointed bow. They turned a ghostly greenish-white color under the surface. I wiggled them. Framed between my hands was a stump. I sat back up. The bottom of the lake surrounding the canoe was covered with stumps. "What's with all the stumps?"

"This is a man-made lake. Back in the fifties, Central Maine Power dammed the river and it formed a lake in this river basin. See how the sides kind of slope up in a natural valley?"

"And they cut down the trees?"

"They cut down the trees, and they moved the village that used to sit in this valley."

"How do you move a village?"

"From what I know of the dam relicensing project, the villagers knew that the dam was imminent and that the power it would supply would be best for Maine. The power company bought the land, and the residents moved their houses to higher ground. There are stories of people putting their houses up on logs and rolling them up the valley."

"This was in the *nineteen* fifties? That just wouldn't happen in California."

"You have to remember, this is rural Maine, and we're talking about bringing electricity into homes."

I squinted into the lake. We floated over a graveyard of tree stumps where people had once walked. I plunged my paddle down to touch one. It was too deep. My spine tensed.

"But what about people's yards?"

"I guess they were just flooded as they were."

I imagined fences outlining yards for nonexistent homes hidden under leagues of water. Flower gardens smothered. Decks abandoned. Trellises swept away. Cracked sidewalks lining deserted roads with unneeded street signs still attached to poles. They couldn't have known how high the water level would climb. Telephone poles jutting up in the middle of the lake. A lone church steeple like the tip of an iceberg. What if people moved their houses, but not to safe-enough ground? Stranded homes would be claimed by the lake. Water rushing into the windows. Floating furniture trapped against the ceiling. Escaped pots and pans bobbing on the surface. Boaters would scrape their outboard motors against a submerged chimney and assume it was a rock.

"We need to move to deeper water where I can't see." I stabbed my paddle into the lake and made strong, hard strokes toward the middle. Lucas took his paddle from across his knees and matched my pace. I eased up only when the surface looked innocuous again.

"Does it bother you that much?" Lucas asked.

"There's just something disturbing about it that I can't explain. A lake is supposed to be a natural body of water. There shouldn't be a town or anything else man-made underneath it. I'd rather just pretend there's nothing to see than think about what might be down there."

"Fair enough," he said. "But what if it's something really cool?" The water dripped off the end of his paddle and ran down his calf, making a wet track in his leg hair. The dog groaned and stretched his legs out straight before relaxing back into his sprawl.

"I think I've had enough discoveries this week." I switched my paddle to my right hand and held out my wrist. "It's my design," I said, "but it's Claire's bracelet. I found it in her jewelry box."

"If you don't mind me asking . . ." Lucas scooted forward in his seat. "How much did you know?"

"It all came out of the blue. One minute I'm cataloging artwork, filling jewelry orders from my website, and planning a trip to Peru with my mother, and the next minute I'm getting a letter from a lawyer telling me my birth mother, who I knew nothing about, died in a car crash and left me all her belongings."

"My God."

"Yeah," I said. "Wasn't there someone else Claire should have left this to? Like your mother, or you? Didn't she have any family?"

"She was married, but her husband died when I was really young. Cancer, I think. After that, she spent holidays with us."

We drifted for a few minutes, neither of us paddling.

"What did your parents say?" Lucas asked.

"They're out of the country. I haven't told them yet." I slid my hands along the length of the canoe paddle feeling the smooth, wet wood under my fingertips.

"Are you still going to Peru?"

I nodded. "We leave in a few weeks." The dog shifted in the bottom of the canoe. Stretching his back out along one side and pushing against the opposite side with his legs. He sighed.

"I'll keep Riley while you're gone," Lucas said. At the sound of his name, the dog lifted an eyebrow. "He's good company for a bachelor like myself." He gave me a sly smile.

I picked up my paddle. "Time to head in?"

We angled back to the dock. A light breeze puffed across the pond, and a pair of iridescent blue dragonflies landed on the bow. All was quiet except for the occasional bumping sounds of our paddles hitting the fiberglass hull and the lap of the water against the side. A mama merganser steered her baby ducklings out of our path to safety. I kept my eyes slightly ahead of us, so the water shimmered a velvet blue. If it weren't for the hidden drowned village, this could have been a scene painted by Winslow Homer.

I hopped out first when we reached the dock and pulled the canoe alongside. The dog threaded himself over the boat and onto the wooden dock. He shook once, the motion starting with his head and working its way down his body and off the tip of his tail like a shockwave. Lucas headed to his truck with the canoe across the expanse of his shoulders. The dog picked up his stick and dropped it at my feet. I flung it toward the water. When Lucas returned, I stood at the end of the dock shading my eyes. The dog stared at the stick at my feet, as if willing it to throw itself. I couldn't pry my eyes from the lake, knowing the villagers' lives were altered irrevocably when they were forced to leave.

"Was Claire's house moved?"

He shrugged. "Could've been."

★ ★ ★

The dog and I watched Lucas's truck disappear down the driveway.

"You wait here," I said and pushed open the door. I didn't see the hanging towel I had hoped for, but the bench seat opened and folded neatly inside were several old towels along with a day pack, some water bottles, and hiking boots. The dog's tail thumped onto the porch when I reemerged. He dove into the towel, wiggling against my hands, and seemed to take the most pleasure when I rubbed his ears dry. He snorted a few times. Sneezed once. And then sat back and held out his front paw. I dried it off. He exchanged it for the other one, then did the back two.

This time when I opened the door, he rushed past me and into the kitchen. His tags clanked against something metal. I found him licking an empty stainless-steel food bowl set on a bone-shaped placemat. I filled his water bowl from the tap first, and he drank a few large gulps, then walked over to the pantry door and stared at it. I opened the door and he walked in and sat in front of a plastic vacuum-sealed container.

"You're no dummy, are you?" Once the dog was inhaling his kibble, I dug around in the pantry and found some instant oatmeal packages, Fig Newmans, and dried apricots.

I munched my makeshift lunch on a bar chair at the center

island. When the dog finished eating, he sprawled at my feet. I felt most at home in the kitchen. I'd only had to open a few drawers before I found a plate and spoon, and I didn't feel as much like I was invading her privacy.

As an only child I'd always had my own space. I had to be clean in the rest of the house, but my bedroom was my own domain. I would build forts out of sheets, securing one end in the dresser drawers, then draping them over my desk chair and tying them to my bedpost to make an elaborate tunnel system from my door to my bed, which would stay up for months. You couldn't walk more than a step inside, but my mother just shut the door and let me do as I pleased. It also had the added benefit of keeping my father out of my room. He thought nothing of reading anything I left on my desk—not to mention seeing how much people put in the church offering basket as it was passed down the pew—and often asked me questions about what he'd uncovered, further frustrating me that he didn't have the decency to hide his poking around.

Even when I babysat, I rarely snooped. I had friends who would go through every drawer, look under the bed for the *Playboys*, check the nightstand for the vibrator, peek in the dresser for lingerie, flip through bills and bank statements, read emails left open on the screen. The worst thing I ever did was dig for the hidden ice cream in the back of the freezer. I always had the sense that snooping could leave me with more than I bargained for. Finding the jewelry had only confirmed this.

My return ticket to California was booked for the next morning. I spent the afternoon sending emails for the gallery, scrolling social media, and sketching out some new jewelry designs. Opting to forgo my nightly Netflix habit since I lacked the wireless password, I downloaded a mystery novel set in Maine and spent a quiet evening reading. After a candlelit soak in the jet tub with vanilla-scented bubbles and the dog sitting patiently waiting for me to get out, I decided to try sleeping in the sleigh bed. The dog had flopped into his bed next to the bedroom fireplace but, as soon as the lights were out, I felt the weight of first one paw and then a second on the side of the bed, then nothing for a few heartbeats except dog breath. Next the mattress dipped as the dog hopped up and settled with his head on the pillow. He pressed his back against the length of my spine and his warmth seeped through my nightshirt. I slept more soundly than I had any night since Chris moved out.

CHAPTER SEVEN

Claire

I had planned to hole up in my dorm room over Thanksgiving, eat boxed macaroni and cheese, and ignore the holiday, but Godfrey announced that renovations to the heating system meant that all students were required to leave campus over the break. I read the unwelcome letter placed in my student mailbox and swore.

"What's wrong?" Will asked.

"I can't stay here over Thanksgiving."

"Then you'll come home with us." Trey slapped shut his postbox and removed his key.

I zipped my mail into my backpack and swung it over my shoulder.

"I can't do that." I started walking to the dining hall to meet Lauren.

"Hold up. Why not? Will's coming. My parents won't care."

I stopped. "I'll just ask Lauren."

"Come," he said. "The Price family loves a good charity case."

★ ★ ★

Lauren pushed her tray along the serving line. "You're really going home to Thanksgiving with the Royals?"

"It wasn't like I planned it."

She stopped and faced me. "Do you know how many people would kill to do that?"

"They're just people. You went to school with them for the last eight years." I grabbed a plated brownie. "I don't understand the big deal."

"That's because you're not from here."

"Whatever." I started walking to a table.

Lauren sat across from me, grinning. "Okay, promise me you'll share all the details."

"I promise."

Her smile faded. "And promise me you won't become one of them."

"Do you think that's happening?"

"You're a good person. Just so closed off," she paused, "understandably."

Lauren and I had covered a lot of both literal and emotional ground on our runs. I had told her in detail about losing my parents, and how I still found myself picking up the phone to call them, or how I could be fine for months and then the littlest thing like a forgotten pair of reading glasses or a flash of color on a passing person's shirt would send me right back into grief.

"Those families have been ruthless for generations," Lauren said.

★ ★ ★

We pulled into the circular pea-gravel driveway of a stately home in Concord, Massachusetts. The Price family estate I had heard so many rumors about was an immense grey colonial with white trim, black shutters, and symmetrical dormer windows. It was not in fact a castle with a moat and fire-breathing dragon, but close. Bare trees stood sentry—rows of grey trunks and spidery branches—having already shed their vibrant fall foliage, and the well-manicured yard stretched back into the woods behind the house. It was midday on the Wednesday before Thanksgiving. Classes had ended the day before, and the three-hour drive had passed more quickly than I wanted, which meant I now stared at the mansion through the backseat window of the parked car.

"Are you coming?" Trey asked.

I opened the car door and pulled my duffle bag from the trunk of his BMW.

"My parents are probably at the club," he said, fitting his key into the lock. The door swung open to reveal a broad, hardwood-floored entryway, a round hall table with a crystal vase of freshly cut flowers, and a grand stairway ascending on the right. "This way."

Will and I tromped up the stairs after Trey. He pointed at doorways. "That's my sister's room. She's doing a year abroad in Italy. Will, take your usual room." He stopped at his bedroom door. "And Claire, you can have that one at the end of the hall. It has its own bathroom."

I pushed the guestroom door open to a bedroom straight from a luxury magazine—a mahogany four-poster bed with a fluffy down comforter and contrasting throw pillows, a matching dresser and nightstand, and a classic striped wing chair. In the bathroom, thick monogrammed towels hung over a heated rack, and a basket housed minibottles of fancy shampoos and soaps like in a high-end hotel. The view out the window overlooked the circular drive below.

I busied myself with unpacking, knowing I would never spend another Thanksgiving with my parents. Even though there were only three of us, our table had expanded to host many of our family friends who contributed their favorite side dishes, so that this mishmash of holiday traditions became our family tradition.

Trey's mother arrived home first. She wore tailored grey-wool slacks, a white blouse, and a navy cardigan knotted over her shoulders. Her silver hair was styled in a simple, yet elegant cut, and she carried herself as if she were balancing a book on her head. She offered her cheek to Trey for a dry kiss, patted Will on the arm, and extended her hand to me.

"We're so happy you could join us," she said. "Especially with my daughter not coming home, I'll appreciate another female in the house. I let our housekeeper enjoy Thanksgiving with her own family."

"Thank you for having me."

She waved a manicured hand. "Any girlfriend of Will's is always welcome."

I wondered who had used the term girlfriend.

She turned to Trey. "Are you hungry? Marie left deviled eggs in the refrigerator."

A car crunched on the gravel driveway and she glanced out the window. "Looks like your father is home from his war games."

I wrinkled my nose at Will.

When the connecting door to the garage opened, in walked a tall, lanky man wearing a Revolutionary War soldier's uniform complete with riding boots, a blue coat with white straps criss-crossed over his chest, and a tricorne hat. I presumed he'd left his musket and bayonet in his Mercedes.

"Trey, my boy, welcome home," his voice boomed in the kitchen. He slapped Trey on the back, shook Will's hand with some kind of elaborate clasp, and turned to me. "You must be Claire." He took my hand in his. "A pleasure, young lady."

"It's nice to meet you, Mr. Price."

"Call me Chaz." He walked over to the liquor cabinet. "Do you drink scotch, Claire?"

"I'm afraid not."

"Why don't you change out of your uniform before you start in on the cocktails," Mrs. Price said.

He poured two fingers of Macallan into three rocks glasses, and handed one to each of the boys before knocking back his own. "Dad's part of the local reenactment group."

"Have you been to the North Bridge?" Mr. Price asked.

"This is my first time to Massachusetts."

"You're in for a treat. The shot heard 'round the world was less than three miles from here. We'll go the day after Thanksgiving."

Trey groaned.

Trey's mother pulled the tray of deviled eggs from the refrigerator. Mr. Price reached for one, but she swatted his hand. "Go clean up first." He popped an egg in his mouth, winked, and headed upstairs, chewing. She turned to me. "Claire, would you like a glass of chardonnay?"

"Thank you," I said, never before having had a glass of chardonnay.

She poured the glass and handed me a monogramed cocktail napkin. "I'm sure your family will miss you this holiday," she said. "Hopefully you'll see them at Christmas."

I took a gulp of wine. I'd assumed Trey would forewarn his parents. "Unfortunately, I'm all that's left of my family."

She blanched. "I'm so sorry. I didn't realize."

"It's all right." My fake smile, automatic.

"Well, we are very pleased to have you join our family this Thanksgiving." She held her glass up to toast and I clinked mine to hers.

★ ★ ★

That night a soft knock sounded on my bedroom door, and in the pause before it cracked open, I wasn't sure who I hoped it would be. Then Will slipped inside, tiptoed across the Berber rug, and slid into bed next to me.

"Are you sure we should be doing this?" I whispered.

"It's a big house; no one heard me," he said. He pulled me to him, and I rested my head on his chest, listening to his steady heartbeat. "I realized today I don't know how your parents died."

"Does it matter?"

"I know so little about you."

"It goes both ways, Will."

He was quiet for a moment. "We need to try harder."

I pulled the sheets up higher. "PanAm crash. It was all over the news, and I was tired of being the girl who lost her parents so publicly. I came here to be anonymous."

"You picked the wrong group of people to hang out with if you want to be anonymous."

"I beg to differ," I said. "There's more misinformation out there about you guys than in the National Enquirer."

★ ★ ★

I spent most of Thanksgiving morning in the comfortable role of Mrs. Price's sous chef, which gave me something to focus on instead of socializing. The males watched Detroit versus the Oilers in the football game on a big-screen television in the family room. Sloan and her family would be joining us for dinner, as would Trey's grandparents. The table was already set with china, crystal, and monogrammed silver that probably came over with the Prices on the Mayflower, as opposed to my mother's hodgepodge of tableware. Calligraphic nameplates assigned us our proper places, alternating boy-girl, mine between Will and Trey, with Sloan on Trey's other side. When the guests arrived, I helped pass hors d'oeuvres and generally made myself useful, a skill that always served me well in other people's homes.

The Caldwells and the senior Prices appeared to be cut from the same cloth as Trey's parents. The men wore sport coats, the women donned pearls, and they all looked as if they should be going on a fox hunt. They introduced me as Will's "California girlfriend from Godfrey," and everyone nodded and made polite conversation. As an only child, I'd spent many hours around adults and could hold my own. I too had grown up at the country club. My father worked in the semiconductor field right out of Stanford and was later recruited to Intel during the infancy of the Silicon Valley, but people who traced their lineage to the Founding Fathers heard the word *California* and made certain assumptions. I let them.

After we were seated at the dining-room table, grace said with bowed heads, and everyone had shared what they were thankful for that year, the talk turned to Godfrey. "So what do you have in the works to retaliate for that prank Alpha Tau pulled?" Sloan's father asked Trey.

"What's this?" Mr. Price asked. He looked at Trey.

"It's nothing," Trey said.

"Nonsense," Mr. Caldwell said. "I heard about it at the club. Rodger Miller was bragging about his son's involvement."

"Rodger always was bit of a bore," Mrs. Price said.

"Trey, my boy, spit it out." Mr. Price's eyes had narrowed.

Trey's mouth tightened. "Alpha Tau kidnapped us at the Halloween reading and dumped us in the woods. Please pass the gravy."

"That's not all I heard," Mr. Caldwell said.

"Daddy," Sloan said. She glared at him.

"What? They should be humiliated if they let this happen."

"We were ambushed," Trey said through clenched teeth.

I placed the gravy in front of him.

"There were fliers of you in only what God gave you all over campus," Mr. Caldwell said.

"Is there no honor code anymore?" Mrs. Price said.

"What?" Trey's father's voice boomed down the table. I

could imagine him commanding his regiment into predestined battle. "Back in our day, a prank was met with a better prank."

"It's different now," Trey said. "We could be expelled." He doused his turkey and potatoes.

"Not with the amount of money I donate to that school."

"Don't be crass, Chaz," Mrs. Price said.

"The prank we played my senior year is legendary. When are you ever going to show them what a Price is made of?"

Trey ignored him.

Charles Price poured another glass of wine and launched into a long tale that, from their reactions, I knew I was the only one at the table who hadn't already heard ad nauseam. One night during Hell Week when all the pledges were assembled in the living room drunk out of their minds, Mr. Caldwell pretended to noisily break in the upstairs window of the house. Mr. Price, as president, told them all to stay put and he would go upstairs to check it out; he made a show of taking one of the hunting guns and ammo out of the locked cabinet. Once upstairs, he and Sloan's father doused the area with stolen meat juice from the dining hall, rolled Mr. Caldwell up in the Oriental rug, and discharged the gun. Mr. Price ran back downstairs and, in what he called his "greatest acting role," pretended he had killed Mr. Caldwell and was terrified of going to jail, ruining his life and the family name. The brothers convinced the pledges to carry the rug-rolled body out of the house and dig a hole to bury him out in the woods.

"You should have seen those pledges. They were blubbering like babies, and one or two of them pissed their pants, but by God they dug that hole." The men laughed as if this was a hilarious skit they witnessed. "We told them, any pledge willing to cover up a murder was worthy of being our brother." Mr. Price raised his glass. "A toast. To the Gentleman, the Scholar, and the Jolly Good Fellow."

I shuddered. My father couldn't have conceived such a scheme, let alone boasted about it with such pride around a holiday table.

Later that night, as I was loading the last of the dishes into the dishwasher after the guests left, I overheard Trey and his father arguing in the den. I couldn't make out all the words, but I could tell that Trey was receiving a violent berating, and the words *family honor*, *upholding tradition*, and *social status* echoed through the walls as his father slammed his hand down on what I assumed was the desk to emphasize his point.

"That story was horrifying," I said to Will in bed. He stared up at the ceiling, cradling his head in his hands.

"I'm not sure you fully understand the pressure we're under from our families."

"Because my parents are dead?" I studied his silhouette.

"You said it yourself, California is different."

"I didn't grow up in a barn."

He sat up. "But you didn't grow up with years of time-honored family tradition. Your whole life hasn't already been planned out for you. You didn't have to go to Exeter, or Godfrey, or make sure that you're a member of all the right clubs and summer in the right places. You can go where you want, be who you want to be."

"No one is holding a gun to your head."

"It's not that easy, Claire."

"It's not that hard either. I know how it feels to have your world turned upside down. You figure it out." I turned away from him and pulled the sheets up to my chin.

★ ★ ★

The next morning I came down to the kitchen in my running clothes. Will and Trey sat at the table drinking coffee. Will looked hungover, and Trey had a black eye and swollen cheekbone. I gave them a quizzical look, but before I could speak Will said, "Going for a run?"

"Yes, want to come?"

"I think I'm coming down with something."

"I'll go with you," Trey said. "Let me change." He went upstairs.

Will pressed his head between his palms.

"What happened?"

"It doesn't concern you. It's better if you just drop it. Trust me."

Trey and I had never run together. We started down the driveway in silence. Our shoes crunched on the gravel driveway, our breathing increased, and the birds squabbled in the trees.

"This way," he said. "Our property backs up to the conservation lands." We turned down a carriage path, and soon we entered a meadow lined by a stone wall and surrounded by dense woods, with trails forking in different directions.

I studied his bruised face out the corner of my eye. "This is pretty," I said.

"Yeah, I spent a lot of time roaming these woods as a kid."

The only times Trey and I had been alone together had been in the tent and the library tower. Sometimes I caught him staring at me when I talked, and I certainly studied him when I thought no one would notice, but we pretended those encounters never happened. I knew the feel of his hands along my body, the fresh scent of his deodorant when he sweat, the hardness of his muscles under his shirt, and the weight of his body on mine. But I had a hard time reconciling the intimacy of those moments with the loose-gaited runner next to me now. I lengthened my stride and sped up a notch. He matched me.

We ran around a lily pad-covered pond, its banks tangled with the bent stalks of golden reeds and cattails.

"See the beaver dam?" Trey said, slowing down. "If you remove some sticks so water trickles, he'll come out and fix it."

"What happens to the beavers when it freezes?"

"They spend the winter inside their lodge."

"Sounds cozy."

We ran along a set of train tracks, tunneling through the trees and then down a slight grade with mountain-bike tire ruts frozen in the dried mud. He pulled up at the edge of a small, crystal-clear lake cradled in the surrounding woods.

He grinned at me. "Walden Pond."

"The Walden Pond?"

"'I went to the woods because I wished to live deliberately.' That Walden Pond."

"Look at you. You're a secret English major."

"Environmentalist."

"If you say so."

"Come on."

We explored Thoreau's cabin site and then walked the trail to the main swimming beach. We sat on the cold, stone steps, shoulder to shoulder, and looked out across the pond. The clear water sparkled the same vibrant blue as Lake Tahoe, reminding me of childhood summers. Trey took my hand without looking at me, lacing his fingers through mine. We sat in silence.

"Are we ever going to talk?" I stared across the water.

"Aren't we talking?"

"Trey." I turned and looked at him, then lightly touched his blackened eye. "That sound wasn't your father's hand hitting the desk, was it?"

He ran his fingers over my knuckles, then lifted my hand to his lips. "My parents really like you. My mom especially."

I covered our joined fingers with my free hand, like paper besting rock. "What are we doing?"

Trey released his grip. "I don't know."

"He's your best friend. Plus there's Sloan."

Trey examined the seam between the stone steps, tracing it with his finger, then stopped and stared at me. We were no longer hidden in the darkness of the tent or by the cloak of the midnight sky.

"I don't know what it is about you, Claire," he said. "I just can't stay away." Trey pulled my face to his, kissed me, then drew back, framing my cheeks between his hands. His hazel eyes shined with flecks of gold. His cheeks sported a day's worth of stubble. Sweat from our run darkened his hair. He stared into me, as if searching for some kind of answer. After Trey kissed me again, my hand pressed to his chest where his heart beat through his damp shirt, we broke apart. He pulled me to my feet and we raced back to the house. Trey won by half a length.

"There you two are," Mrs. Price flipped a sizzling piece of bacon in the cast-iron pan. "How many pancakes do you want?" Mr. Price sat at the breakfast table, legs crossed at the ankle, glasses balanced on the end of his nose, sipping coffee and reading the *New York Times*.

"Where's Will?" I asked.

"Back in bed," Mrs. Price said.

Mr. Price looked over the top of his glasses. "I think he's just trying to get out of our trip to Minute Man National Park. Eat up, we have a big day of history ahead of us."

★ ★ ★

On the way home to school, I stared at the backs of Will's and Trey's heads from the leather rear seat of the BMW. The Royals. Some of what they said was true. They were smart, they came from wealth, and things came easily to them—academics, sports, popularity. They were also aloof and insular, and the same rules did not apply. But as kind as the Prices had been to me, that house breathed expectations, it demanded conformity, and it prospered on obedience.

I had promised Will I would try harder. I had promised myself I would not succumb to Trey again. I had promised Lauren

I would not become one of them. Promises can be so hard to keep.

Over the next several weeks, key members of the football team were found naked and duct-taped—derogatory epitaphs inked on their bodies—to high-traffic locations all over campus—the dining hall, the central flagpole, the chapel pulpit, the grand library staircase, the stage at the student center. Many photos were taken and spread around campus for those who missed the live viewing. No one was caught for the retaliation, but everyone knew who was behind it.

CHAPTER EIGHT

Claire

M aine is dark in winter. The sun sets at four o'clock in the afternoon. During Godfrey's Dead Week, the sports stopped, the parties ceased, and everyone holed up to study for their exams, emerging only to eat and sleep, if that. Godfrey was not one of those schools that allowed students to drop classes up until the last day. They prided themselves on rigorous academics, and rigorous academics they delivered. The Godfrey library with its proud clock tower and beaming light stood as the centerpiece of campus. The four-story building not only housed the library; it also held the English and History Departments, as well as several small bookshelf-lined seminar rooms furnished with heavy oak tables and chairs bearing the Godfrey crest to encourage lively discussion. The ground floor, known as "the tunnel," served as a cut-through from one side of campus to the other—a particularly important passage during winter when I needed to defrost between my dorm room and the Student Center. One entered the main library on the first floor into a light and airy atrium that stretched the full height of the building and contradicted the labyrinth of stacks and warrens of dark hidden passageways reached by a grand spiral staircase.

I heard the cry "Day-o, day-o" echo through the atrium from my study spot deep in the stacks. Putting down my Russian History notes, I went to the balcony overlooking the first floor. There, in a circle with their pitch pipe, stood Looking for Treble, singing The Banana Boat Song and dancing their ridiculous steps. More students emerged from the maze of study carrels, drawn to the voices like moles blinking into the sunlight. I rested against the balcony railing on folded arms watching Trey, Will, and the other members of the a cappella group break up the monotony of finals. When they looked up, I waved and both boys smiled. Looking for Treble sang three songs and then bowed to warm applause. I met Will and Trey at the bottom of the staircase as they pulled on their coats.

"You guys do this every year?"

"Yeah, it's a tradition," Trey said.

"Do you want to meet up later?" Will asked.

"I'm in for a long night," I said. "I have a Russian History exam tomorrow and two annoying fifty-page papers due by the end of the week."

"How about tomorrow?"

"We could go for a run in the early afternoon, before it gets dark?"

"It's a date," Will said. "Have fun studying."

I headed back to my hideout and lost myself in the Bolshevik Revolution until long after the library closed. I was busy memorizing key dates in the rise of Lenin and the Communist Party when Trey appeared around the end of the stack.

"I thought you might still be here," he said.

"It's late." I looked at my watch. "How'd you get in?"

"Same way I did before."

"Yeah, you never told me how you got in before."

"Let's just say that I inherited a key."

"Of course you did."

He sat down on the arm of my leather reading chair and crossed his arms. "You're not afraid here by yourself?"

"I'm locked in. Who else but you is going to come get me?"

"But you're alone in this cavernous building."

"How can I be alone with so many books?"

"You really are a nerd, you know?" He took my Russian History book out of my hands and set it aside.

"Why are you here?" I asked.

"Isn't it obvious?"

"Trey."

He pushed a stray piece of hair back behind my ear and let his fingers linger on my cheek. He pulled me to him and his hands were in my hair, and my back was against the books, and we sank to the ground, entangled in each other in the darkness of the musty stacks. Afterward, I lay with my head on his chest, running my fingers down the length of his arm, feeling his smooth skin while he played with my hair.

"You're like an illicit drug," he said.

"That's what it is, isn't it? That I'm off limits?" I sat up and reached for my shirt, tossing his pants to him.

"Maybe," he said. "But explain the tent."

I paused. "I thought I dreamt it."

"It's like something else takes over. Something I can't stop."

I watched him button the fly of his jeans.

"What?" he said.

"I don't think I want you to stop."

★ ★ ★

Sloan found me the next day in the women's locker room after my run with Will. She wore running tights, a long-sleeved t-shirt, down vest, and knit hat, still managing to emit a sexual radiance, whereas I just looked tired and sweaty in a similar outfit. She sat on the empty bench next to my locker in the area reserved for the track team.

"I didn't think you played a winter sport," I said.

"What are you doing for winter break?"

"Staying on campus. And you?" I dug inside my locker for my keys and student ID.

"You really don't have any family? Not even grandparents?"

"None that are living."

She crossed her arms over her chest. "The Prices seemed to really like you."

I stopped searching in my locker and looked at her. "It was a nice Thanksgiving."

"What about Will?"

"What about him?"

She leaned her head back against the metal lockers. "Why don't you go home with him?"

"Because I want to stay here." I shut my locker door and grabbed my bag.

Sloan stayed put on the bench.

"Are you coming?" I asked.

"I lied before," she said.

"About?"

"That sometimes I look the other way." Sloan paused. Stared at me. "It's not true."

"Okay." I stood in the doorway, my gym bag slung over my shoulder.

"Trey's been distracted this year."

I hitched the bag higher on my shoulder. "He loves you."

She picked at her running tights. "But is he *in* love with me?"

"Will's waiting for me," I said.

"I'm sorry," Sloan said. She looked at her hands in her lap. "I don't really have anyone else to talk to about this."

"You have lots of friends." I stared back at her.

"It's different." She met my eyes. "I don't have to pretend with you." Sloan shrugged. "Because you don't really matter."

I stepped out the door without her.

★ ★ ★

Everyone cleared out after the last finals, leaving behind an abandoned campus covered in a blanket of white, like a perfect quaint New England college tucked inside a snow globe. The falling snow muffled all sounds, and I walked the paths between my dorm and the Student Center appreciating the quiet emptiness I never experienced during the semester. I had borrowed a pair of cross-country skis and a map of local trails from the Outing Club before they closed for the holiday and planned to spend my break exploring the miles of ski trails and working my way through the stack of novels on my nightstand.

It was my third Christmas as an orphan. My parents had been on their way home from London for the holidays, and the news of their deaths is forever linked to carols, colored lights, ornaments, eggnog, and holiday cheer. Last year I went to a friend's home, but trying to fit into another family's traditions felt lonelier than being alone. Plus, as an only child in a house where each of us could be in our own space without hearing the others, dorm living—the shared bathrooms, the noisy hallways, people leaving their doors wide open to visitors—felt congenial, but also suffocating. I needed time alone.

I skied the campus arboretum trails we ran on all fall, the naked trees with their spindly branches both familiar and new in their dusting of snow. Christmas morning I threw my skis in Lauren's Outback, brushed snow off the windshield, scraped the ice with my student ID, blasted the heat, and set off to Lone Loon Pond. A solo morning ski through a pure winter landscape felt like a peaceful and cleansing new holiday tradition.

No longer blocked by thick deciduous leaves, the panoramic view of the lake opened up in the winter to reveal pine and spruce sprinkled between the bare maple and birch trunks. A sign at the campground documented the relocation of the town that once sat in this valley before the river was dammed to bring electric power to the region and Lone Loon Pond was formed. I clicked into my skis, slid past the picnic tables and half-buried campfire ring, and followed the tracks to the shore. Lone Loon Pond stretched before me, a frozen sheet of white. Camps—as I had learned cabins were called in Maine—dotted the shoreline, their docks removed for the winter. Multiple ski tracks led to the middle of the frozen lake, crisscrossing the expanse, but I hugged the shoreline trail, not trusting the ice.

About half the camps appeared to be summer homes, and the others looked winterized, snowmobiles parked in the driveways, enormous piles of stacked wood, and smoke curling from the chimneys, like the picture on the Log Cabin maple syrup. A cozy, wintery feel that made me want to sit by the fire with a grilled-cheese sandwich, tomato soup, and a good book.

I began to imagine myself living on Lone Loon Pond, skiing with my dog, reading by the fireplace, growing a vegetable garden in the summer. Solitude, but a town and college nearby. My skis made a satisfying swish through the tracked snow, the icy cold burned my cheeks, and the incredible quiet of the wilderness welcomed me. I hadn't expected to feel so at home in Maine. I appreciated the taciturn nature of the locals, and the way everyone spent so much time outdoors. People looked out for each other in a way that felt familiar. California had its six-foot fences and, as long as you didn't bother anyone, people were friendly enough but minded their own business. In Maine, they might not have a lot to say, but when they did it was important, and they would be the first to pull your car out of a snow bank. I felt a kindred spirit with the skier who carved the tracks before me, as I traced his or her path along the lakeshore.

I settled into the steady, gliding rhythm of my skis, the snow squeaking beneath them, and the tension from the end of the semester finally began to ease from my shoulders. My nose dripped and my exposed earlobes stung. I pulled my wool hat lower and soon warmed from exertion. Physical exercise had helped me through the loss of my parents and the subsequent months of well-meaning friends trying to cajole me back to life. I ran alone, deadened, covering the distance. One foot in front of the other, in my own form of meditation, until exhausted. Time had dampened my grief but hadn't erased it. Now there was simply before, when I believed nothing truly bad could happen, and after, when I knew it could. That night in the tent and each subsequent encounter with Trey were the only times I had let myself fully *feel* since losing my parents, and I didn't know why.

The boughs of the pine trees bent with the burden of heavy snow, and my poles struck the solid ice hidden under the soft blanket of white as I propelled myself forward. I came around a blind curve into a cove thick with willow bushes poking through the snow. At first I didn't see him blending into the woods. Then, as if he'd decided to reveal himself like a magician, there stood a moose with a thick winter coat, whiskers on his nose, and a full rack of majestic antlers. I froze in my tracks and watched him. The snow came halfway up his light-socked knees, and his beard moved as he chewed a mouthful of willows. He tilted his large ears toward me. For a long moment, longer than felt natural, his earnest brown eyes locked onto mine as if to transfer his strength and grace to me. Willing me to remember who I once was. He slowly blinked his long lashes, breaking the spell, and stretched his neck to take another bite. It was the best Christmas gift I could have asked for.

★ ★ ★

A few days later, I was snuggled under the covers in my plaid flannel pajamas and ski hat reading my novel when a bold knock interrupted me. No one was due back on campus for another week. I padded across the small room in my wool L.L.Bean socks and cracked the door open.

"Surprise," Trey said, his cheeks flushed red from the cold.

"What are you doing here?"

"I thought I'd come back to campus a little early."

"What about your family?"

"They think I'm skiing." He cocked his head to the side. "Which I plan to be."

I stepped aside and let him into my room. He took off his coat and unwound the scarf from his neck.

"Seriously. Why are you here?" I asked. "Did something happen at home?"

"Are you not happy to see me?"

I sat down cross-legged on my bed and studied him. He moved gingerly. "I'm happy to see you," I said.

"Good." Trey closed the distance between us, pushing me back onto the twin. "Then make some room in that little bed for me."

Trey and I spent the next week secluded in our own private winterland. We skied, ate, slept, read, had sex, and talked, never straying from each other's side. I didn't care about Sloan, or Will, or what any of it meant. We just lived as if we were the only two people who mattered. Unable to hide the new bruises, he told me his father had gone ballistic when Trey said he didn't plan to join his finance firm after graduation. His mother begged him, for everyone's sake, to clear out for a few days.

CHAPTER NINE

Lindsay

When I arrived home from Maine, I immediately texted Emily, *PBA*, the code a relic from our childhood. Both only children, we'd developed a club called the Parents Bamboozling Association that we were co-presidents of, and whose membership was restricted to our pets. The goal of the club was straightforward, to get what we wanted out of our parents, and most of our meetings focused on inventive ways to do that.

Emily didn't waste any time. *C napping, M preschool. Forget shower. Come over & play.*

Not wanting to wake the baby, I knocked softly on the front door and pushed it inward without waiting for her to answer. The house looked wrecked by an earthquake. Toys were scattered everywhere. Books had been pulled off the shelves. I had to step over an overturned dining room chair to make it down the hall. The daughter of strict parents, Emily had swung the pendulum to the opposite extreme.

When I'd moved back to the Bay Area and wanted to meet people, I'd suggested we start a book group with her friends.

"You become more like your mother every day," she'd told me.

"Please don't remind me."

Our first few book group meetings were all about drinking too much wine, eating rich foods, complaining about men, and remembering somewhere along the way to talk about the book. And then Emily became pregnant. Wine became mineral water. We no longer served brie or any other soft cheese. Sushi was out of the question. Not to mention caffeine. Emily began to quote baby blogs as if they were the absolute authority on everything from religion to politics and managed to steer every conversation back to what was happening with her body.

Before Emily, pregnancy was only a concept. But she made me realize that someone—someone whom I'd never met—thought of me every waking moment for nine months. Had my mother changed her eating habits? Did she cry like Emily when her favorite jeans stopped fitting? Did she lie awake at night singing to me and waiting to feel me kick inside her? When I was wondering what presents I would receive for my birthday, was she questioning what had become of me? After Emily had her baby and focused her attention on raising her new daughter, the questions had faded—until now.

I found Emily loading the dishwasher with dirty breakfast dishes. The kitchen opened into what she referred to as The Great Room. I sat on my customary bar stool at the island separating the two spaces. She set a coffee mug in front of me.

"Ok, spill it," she said. "Are you still trying to get a pony?"

"In a nutshell?" I said. "My birth mother was killed in a car accident. I just went to see the house she left me in Maine. My parents get home tomorrow, and I'm about to spend a week alone in Peru with my mother."

"What?" Emily's mouth dropped open, and her hand holding a sippy cup froze above the dishwasher.

"Oh, and did I mention the dog I now own and the really hot neighbor?"

The baby monitor crackled on the counter as Connor coughed in his sleep. Emily didn't even look at it.

"Why didn't you call me immediately?"

"Telling you would have made it real."

"But it is real."

"Yeah, *real* real," I said. "She had my jewelry."

"She was tracking you. When you have a child, it changes you." Her eyes turned dreamy and I clenched my teeth.

"What I need to decide is how much I tell my parents."

"Why wouldn't you just tell them? Your mother has always been open with you about your adoption."

"I know. My first reaction was to call her, but now after being in Maine it just doesn't feel right," I said. "They raised me. They're my parents, not Claire. Leaving me a house doesn't change that."

"But she gave birth to you. If you had kids, you'd understand."

I set my coffee cup down harder than necessary. It rang against the counter. "Not everyone wants to be a mother."

"They would if they knew how fulfilling it was." Emily turned her back on me and continued to load the dishwasher.

"What about my mother?"

"It's not the same."

"That's not fair, Emily."

Emily shuffled some cups on the top rack to make room for one more coffee mug. She turned to face me. "You don't know what it's like to have a child."

I hid my scowl behind my coffee mug. "I certainly know what it's like to have a mother. Grace Williams is my mother whether she birthed me or not. You're the one who always accuses me of being exactly like her. Just because you don't want to be like your mother doesn't mean I mind being like mine."

Emily stuck out her tongue at me. I scrunched up my nose at her.

After Emily and I pushed Conner down the street in the stroller to pick up Madison from preschool, we came back to the park next to her house to watch them play.

"What would you do if you didn't tell your parents?" Emily asked.

"Sell the house?"

Madison pushed Connor on the swing set. "Have you considered living there?" Emily asked. "It sounds like a pretty incredible place."

"This is ridiculous," I said. "I'm thirty years old. It shouldn't matter."

"It shouldn't, but I'm not surprised," Emily said. "Remember health class?"

In the eighth grade, my health teacher told us to anonymously write a secret on a piece of paper. She retyped them, so no handwriting could be recognized, and put them in a fishbowl where we drew a secret and read it to the class. We were supposed to say reassuring things to the ones that "spoke to us." I had calculated that the best way to pretend it was not *my* secret was to give advice to "the writer" when my secret was read. It would be obvious if I only spoke about my own, so I would have to talk about others. To the person who said they still wet the bed, I offered that we all have something we're embarrassed about and you couldn't help it. To the person who admitted they threw up after every meal, I suggested there were better ways to lose weight, like playing sports. One by one my classmates went to the front of the room and drew a secret out of the fishbowl. Until only one remained.

I watched Josh Rayburn, the most popular boy in class, saunter to the front of the room in his hoodie and camouflage cargo pants, dip his hand dramatically in the bowl, and wiggle his fingers back and forth until they closed around the last piece of paper. He cleared his throat and then read in a deep, strong voice, the envy of most junior-high boys, "My father is an alcoholic and I wish he'd do something about it." I had been so sure that he would read my words, "Sometimes my father drinks too much alcohol and my family pretends he doesn't," that I almost didn't recognize my own secret. And then I felt my cheeks flush. My teacher had changed my sentence. I was so shocked that I couldn't even raise my hand to give myself some fake advice and was still upset enough moments later that I could barely focus on the stories other kids were telling about their parents getting drunk. I forced an impassive expression on my face, slowed my breathing, assumed the look of indifference I'd perfect during my teenage years, and realized my teacher was right. There was a word for it, a word that applied to many people. We just hadn't said it aloud.

Connor and Madison chased each other around the play structure in a game of tag. "You know how your mother likes to keep up the perfect-family facade. You're obeying her unspoken request to play along, just like you always have," Emily said.

I rubbed my forehead. "And?"

"If you admit one truth, what else will you have to acknowledge?"

I dug for my keys in my purse, then pointed them at my parked car, clicking the fob to unlock the doors.

"Tell your mother," Emily said. I headed across the grass to my car. "Love you," she called after me.

"Love you too," I said, waving over my head and not looking back.

If an earthquake cracks the foundation of a house, even if the damage can't be seen, eventually that person will find themself standing in a pile of rubble.

★ ★ ★

The return address of Wilson & Cabot on the large manila envelope announced its presence like a flare gun. I shoved it in a drawer and opened every other piece of mail including the credit card offers and solicitations that I routinely placed in the recycling bin without a second glance. I paid all my bills. Switched my laundry to the dryer. Made a grocery list. Texted

Emily. Checked my email. Wiped down the counters and the table—even though I hadn't eaten on them. Brewed coffee. Drank one cup and poured myself a second. Sighed. Slid open the drawer. Removed the manila envelope, and headed outside to open it at my deck table.

It just contained my copies of the signed papers. At the time, Mr. Cabot's explanation of each document required I only read closely enough to understand the gist before affixing my signature. Now I held the exact details of Claire Sullivan's life-insurance payoff, the appraised value of the house, the account numbers and financial histories of the investments, and various other legal documents detailing the distribution of her will. It was more than I realized. Even without selling the farmhouse, I could afford a down payment in the Bay Area. I could visit the world's best art museums. I could quit my gallery job and travel for the next year in search of inspiration for new jewelry designs and still be able to live comfortably when I returned. It was like winning the lottery, except half didn't evaporate to taxes. I drained my coffee cup and the caffeine buzzed my veins. My hands shook slightly.

I called Lucas. He assured me that Riley was doing well and Beverly was looking after the house. "Are you coming back here soon?" he asked.

The caffeine buzz ground to a halt. It was more like winning *Survivor*. Sure, you got the million dollars, but at the cost of being known as a reality-TV star for the rest of your life.

"I don't know," I said. "I'll give you a call when I figure out my plans. Thank you," I emphasized. "You're a lifesaver," and hung up before I could hear his reply.

★ ★ ★

My mother had managed to keep from me how many shots I would need to visit Peru until it was too late to back out. At my doctor's appointment, the receptionist gave me a clipboard with four pages to fill out and gestured to the empty seats in the sterile waiting room. I sat among strategically placed boxes of Kleenex and bottles of hand sanitizer and started at the top of the form, but stopped short for the first time at the words *Family Medical History.* The receptionist looked at me over the top of her glasses.

"Do you need some water?" she asked.

I bit down hard on the end of the pen I hadn't realized I'd been gnawing.

"Thank you. I'm all right." I extracted the pen from my mouth, wrote the word *adopte*d on the form, and flipped it over for my signature. What did I really know? A name. A location. That she was killed in a car accident instead of by a hereditary disease. I'd always had to accept that what was going to happen to me, was going to happen to me. I had no roadmap to my future. No indication if I was predisposed to breast cancer or heart disease or poor eyesight. When my friends complained they had inherited their mother's thighs, I couldn't join the conversation. I had no idea where my dimples or dark hair or blue eyes had come from. But now I might, and that was only the beginning. It was like being given the chance to be genetically tested, except this wasn't science. It was nature.

★ ★ ★

My parents called when they returned from their barge trip, catching me in the middle of making dinner. Rather than being forever destined to survive on prepackaged meals and takeout, I had decided to learn to cook. It wasn't going so well, but I refused to surrender.

"The house is still standing and the plants seem to have survived," my mother said. "Did we miss anything?"

I hesitated, my knife tip resting on an onion. Telling them

now felt more disloyal than waiting until I knew what I wanted to say. My mother was the one who taught me that words had meaning. To always think before I spoke.

"Not a thing."

"We were gone almost a month."

I stopped slicing onions and dabbed the corner of the dishtowel against my tearing eyes. It smelled funky, like old cheese.

"Let's see, I got my hair cut, prepared some paintings to be loaned to the MOMA, made some new jewelry pieces, went to the beach, you know, the usual."

"So there is nothing you want to tell me?" she asked.

I pressed my lips together, calculating. I'd taken the lawyer's letter with me and returned the adoption folder to their file cabinet. Daniel was no worse for wear after being checked into the kitty hotel for a few days.

"Is there something you're getting at?"

"I have book group tomorrow."

I threw up my hands and the dishtowel landed on the counter. When my friends and I went to college, our mothers started a book group, claiming it was their way of staying in touch now that they no longer had the PTA. It didn't take long for the book group to become infamous among my friends. You'd think they had nothing better to do than gossip about their children. Each month my mother phoned me full of information, as the ladies took a certain pride in out-doing each other. After one, my mother accused me of scoring the winning goal in an intramural soccer game and not telling her.

"I felt ridiculous that Jane knew you'd won the game and I didn't."

"Isn't the point of a book group to read books?" I asked.

"Don't be silly, Lindsay," she said.

"Sorry Mother, nothing for you to report to book group." I turned the oven on to preheat and went back to chopping.

"Maybe it's time for you to meet someone new," she said. My knife hovered above the cutting board. I set it down for fear of nicking my finger along with the onion. I'd met Chris one nostril-freezing winter day when he came into the gallery to get out of the cold. He wasn't wearing gloves or a hat. His scalp shone bright pink through his light blond hair. I offered him a cup of coffee and learned he was earning his masters in engineering at MIT. By the end of the afternoon, I had a schematic drawing on the back of a gallery brochure of how winglets increase efficiencies in airplanes, and he had my phone number. The last time my mother and I talked about my relationship, one of her friend's children had announced they were engaged and she had taken it as an opportunity to ask if Chris and I were planning to marry soon. I had tested answers to that question so many times my practiced response slipped from my lips.

"Since we aren't planning on having any children, there doesn't seem to be any rush." This silenced most people, but that time it silenced me. Wishing I could see her expression instead of interpreting her breathing, I had continued, "I mean I realize I'm an only child, and this means you won't be a grandmother."

"If I really wanted to increase my chances for lots of grandchildren, I could have adopted more kids," she'd said.

"That's pragmatic."

"You know I find my friends who only talk about their grandchildren as dull as you find your friends who talk of nothing but motherhood. There's more to life than raising children."

"Yes, but obviously you wanted children enough to go through the process of adopting me. That's not something you do on a whim."

"Of course," she said. "But too many generations of women were expected to be wives and mothers. I'm happy that you're of a generation who can choose."

In today's phone conversation, after I'd mumbled something

noncommittal, my mother said, "I'm seeing Eileen tomorrow. How's the house hunting?"

"On pause."

"Oh dear. We should have bought you something years ago, but we didn't know how long you'd be here, and of course we thought prices couldn't possibly go any higher, but then hindsight is twenty-twenty and . . ."

"Mom. Stop. Just tell her to give me a call."

★ ★ ★

Eileen snuck up on me in the grocery store as I squeezed avocados. "Lindsay!" She startled me. "I saw your mother at book group. She stressed that we need to find you a house."

"Did she?" I placed a semifirm avocado in my basket.

"I have just the place for you. It's in your neighborhood and oozes character." She used her perky realtor tone, which would make even the worst news, like termite-infested, sound like a good thing. "Can you see it this afternoon?"

"I'm not sure."

"Lindsay." Eileen switched to the stern tone my mother uses. "This could be the house. We don't want someone else to snap it up, now do we?" She looked over her glasses at me. "If you like it, we should put in an offer tonight."

Shifting my shopping basket from one arm to the other, I looked at my watch. "I have lunch plans . . ."

"Good, you can see it after lunch." Eileen started to wheel her cart away. "It's right around the corner from where you live, on Hanover between College and California," she said over her shoulder. "I'll meet you there at two o'clock."

I watched her retreating form longer than necessary before hitching my grocery basket up on my hip and finishing my shopping. I'd barely put my groceries in the fridge before it was time to meet Emily for lunch.

Emily had both Madison and Connor in tow. I deflated. I had hoped to have a serious conversation. They waited out front of the restaurant and didn't see me at first. Madison spun in circles on the sidewalk watching her dress fill out in a ring calling, "Mommy, Mommy, watch me."

Connor tugged on Emily's hand in the other direction and whined, "Mommy, you *have* to. You just *have* to." Emily divided her attention between them.

The thought of having not one, but two beings that needed me to provide absolutely everything for them, on their time frame, was too much. Not to mention her husband, who functioned like a third child, just like Chris had. Before Emily had real children, we used to complain over a bottle of wine how we had to do everything for our significant others and wondered how they'd gotten as far in life as they had. "But they weren't on their own," I'd say. "They went from their mother's care, to college, to us. They've never had to do anything for themselves."

I blamed Chris's mother. My mother wouldn't have tolerated his behavior. Dishes weren't left out at our house. Cabinets and drawers were closed when you finished retrieving what you needed. Towels were rehung on the rack, not left on the bed or the wooden furniture to dry. Not that I was punished. My mother just wouldn't put up with it and made me complete whatever action she felt I had left undone. I often did whatever she wanted scowling, with my arms crossed and dragging my feet, but it never occurred to me to disobey.

"Lindsay!" Madison stopped spinning. She ran to me and bear-hugged my legs. Emily slung Connor into her arms and came our direction.

"We have to talk," I told Emily over Madison's head. After we were seated, and the kids were occupied eating butter straight out of the package and coloring on the paper placements, I said,

"My mother's gotten Eileen to redouble her efforts at finding me a house. Do you think she could have—"

"Mommy! Madison took my crayon." Connor whined. There were ten others to choose from.

"Did not," screamed Madison.

"Did too," screeched Conner.

I shoved a green crayon at Conner. My spine tingled from his high-pitched voice.

"Do both of you want a time-out?" Emily asked in an even tone.

I wanted to smack them but gritted my teeth instead.

"What were you saying?" she asked me.

"Do you think my mother could have found out?"

"Aren't you missing the point here?" Emily grabbed my hands across the table. "Aren't you curious about your birth mother? Don't you want to know why she gave you up and why she left her house to you?"

"Of course," I took my hands back and crossed them in front of me. "But why go stirring up the past when it can't be changed? There's no guarantee I'll find the answers and, until I received that letter from the lawyer, I never gave it much thought. I have parents, and they love me."

"Ouch!" screamed Conner. The other patrons were staring at us. My mother would have already had me by the arm and halfway out of the restaurant.

"No, no, Madison." Emily said, and gave her a jam packet to eat. Madison grinned as if she'd gotten away with murder. "Can't you see you've been given a gift?"

"I like my life the way it is."

"But this could make it better."

"Or worse," I said.

Despite my better judgment, I asked Emily to come see the house for sale. We buckled the kids into their car seats and drove the short distance we would have walked without them.

"Which one is it?" asked Emily.

"I assume the one with the For Sale sign in front. Go slowly, I'll tell you when I see it."

"There it is," Madison called from the back seat. She was right. Emily pulled the car to the curb in front of a cute little Craftsman-style cottage with a white fence and a red door.

"This is more like it," I said. "Are you sure we're at the right house?" I looked up and down the street. "There isn't another for-sale sign on this street?"

"Isn't that your mom's friend?" Emily said, pointing at Eileen pulling up. We parked in front of the gate.

"I don't want to get out of the car," Connor yelled and threw one of his shoes into the street.

"Just leave him," I said.

"I can't do that." Emily said.

"Why not?"

"Something might happen to him."

"He's strapped in."

Emily glared at me.

I shrugged.

"Well?" Eileen asked. She stood with her hands on her hips waiting for us.

"The outside's cute," I said. "But what does it look like inside?"

"Follow me." Eileen swung the gate open with a smug smile. "You'll see that there's a nice little front yard here for a garden and it's fenced in, in case you decide to have a dog."

Emily poked me in the ribs. "Why would you think I want a dog?" I asked.

"You never know, I just like to point out all the positive qualities of a house," Eileen said brightly. Eileen removed the lock box from the front door and pushed it inward so we could enter first. I stepped inside, followed by Madison, and prepared my mental checklist. Emily went back to wrestle Connor from the car. The cottage had nice hardwood floors and a high ceiling that gave it a light, airy feeling. A small living room with a fireplace and built-in bookshelves lay off to the left, and a picture window looked out over the front garden. To the right was a dining room that fit my requirement of being able to hold a table for eight. Through a swinging door off the dining room sat a small but well-organized updated kitchen. It didn't have the newest brushed-steel appliances, but it also didn't have an olive-green fridge or orange shag carpet like I'd seen in plenty of fixer-uppers. A small room that would make a great office stood just off the living room, and at the back of the house the bedroom opened up to a refinished deck and backyard.

"There's space for a hot tub," Eileen said. Apparently, I wasn't the only one reviewing my checklist. "I think you'll be interested in the garage." She grinned like the Cheshire Cat.

When Emily found us in the backyard, Conner was wearing both shoes and stuffing a chocolate chip bribe into his mouth. A stone pathway led to a stand-alone building that from the front looked like a traditional garage but, on the side, solid walls were replaced by large sliding doors that could be opened so the indoor and outdoor spaces merged.

"The woman who lived here gardened," Eileen said. "And converted this into a gardening cottage, but I thought it might be the ideal place for your jewelry workshop." There was a full sink, acres of counters to spread across, and lots and lots of storage.

"Wow!" said Madison.

"Cool," said Emily.

"How much?" I asked.

"It's in your range," Eileen replied. "Admit you like it."

"If I didn't have kids," Emily said. "This is exactly the house I'd want. Do you want to switch lives?"

"You're not helping."

"I'm not kidding," Emily said.

"Shall we put in an offer?" Eileen asked.

"When do I have to decide?" I fingered the faucet handle on the gardening sink.

"Tonight would be best."

I turned the handle, and the water rushed down the drain. I shut it off. Maine had only been a few days ago, and Robert Cabot's letter less than a week before. And although it felt like a lifetime had passed, I had barely broken up with Chris. I turned the faucet again, but this time adjusted the flow to a light trickle, then down to small drops until it squeezed shut and stopped.

"Give me until the morning to think about it," I said.

"Are you sure?" Eileen asked. "We can go straight to my office to fill out the paperwork. I can give you a ride home afterward."

I felt Emily's stare. "Thanks, Eileen," I turned away from the sink to face her. "I appreciate it." I reached down for Madison's hand and pulled her to the front door.

Eileen wore the expression of someone who has just gotten a piece of gum stuck to the bottom of her shoe. "If you change your mind, call me tonight and we can draw up the papers."

"I promise," I said, over my shoulder. I told Emily I would walk home, hugged her then Madison, patted Connor's head, and started down the street. Normally I loved my neighborhood, but now I saw the houses crowded together, an odd mix of small cottages and McMansions. Of course most Silicon Valley types don't want yards. They don't have time to spend on the upkeep of a garden, and if they did have one a fleet of gardeners attended to the grounds. It was no longer the sleepy town where I grew up. They still had the pet parade down Main Street every year where all the children walked, rode, or pulled their pets along behind them in cages, but now the wealth was ludicrous and the children entitled and insatiable. I still hoped for The Big One to send people back to wherever they came from. The only reason I was able to consider buying a house was I had savings, a steady income, and my parents as back-up, so the bank was willing to prequalify me for an irresponsible amount of money.

When I returned home, I shut the door and pressed my forehead against the solid wood between me and the world. I closed my eyes and appreciated the stillness of the air inside the safety of my house. Maybe slightly jet-lagged from Maine, I needed a nap. I crawled into bed and tucked my comforter around me, but I couldn't get comfortable. I tossed and turned. Wrestled the covers. Flipped from my back, to my side, to my stomach. The comforter felt heavy on my legs, and the sheets twisted around my feet, trapping me in one position. I punched my pillow, trying to shape it, but that was no help. Finally I collapsed from exhaustion and dreamt I was standing at the tip of the Maine dock in SCUBA gear. The water of Lone Loon Pond glowed a beautiful tropical blue like in the Caribbean, but when I squinted the shadow of a sunken town emerged from the depths. My phone squawked by my head and I reached out and grabbed it.

"Did you love the house?" my mother asked.

"How did you find out about the house?" The image of the pond still lurked in the shadowy corners of my mind.

"Eileen told me, of course."

"Eileen?"

"Did I wake you up?"

I shook my head to clear the grogginess. "Yeah."

"You know, if you take some ginseng you'll pep right up."

"Are you calling for a reason?"

"I want to know how you liked the house Eileen showed you this afternoon." My mother enunciated each word. "She told me how many places she's shown you already, and you haven't liked any of them. Are you setting your expectations too high? You can always redo a kitchen or relandscape you know. Eileen said it was perfect for you."

"It is perfect for me."

"So what're you waiting for? We're leaving for Peru in a week. Your father and I could help you with a down payment. Do you need us to write you a check?" My parents had bought their own house back in the decades before it became implausible for a school teacher to afford a family home in the Bay Area, and when my grandfather died my father inherited half of the family's Southern California construction company now run by his brother, who seemed to have a never-ending list of celebrity clients.

"No. Please. That's very generous, but I just need to nap. I'll call you tomorrow." I heard "ginseng" and "green tea" as I hung up.

★ ★ ★

Sometime around three in the morning, wide awake and unable to return to sleep, I slipped out the front door and into the cool stillness of the night. Letting the full moon be my guide, I strolled the few short neighborhood blocks engulfed in the symphonic hum of crickets and the sweet scent of night-blooming jasmine. When I reached the white picket fence and red door, I pushed open the gate and made my way to the backyard. I sat against the rough patchwork trunk of the large sycamore tree and stared into its lacy leaves. This was the exact house I had been looking for. Yet another in Maine called to me.

CHAPTER TEN

Lindsay

I had dreaded telling my mother I planned to break up with Chris, but I thought she should hear it from me instead of her book group. "Can we have dinner alone?" I'd asked over the phone. "There's something I want to talk to you about without Dad."

"Well, I don't know," she said. "He'll want to come."

"Mother," I sighed. "You know, some families consider it normal for mothers and daughters to do things alone together."

"What would I say to him?"

"You're an inventive woman. I'm sure you'll think of something."

My mother left me a voicemail naming the time and her favorite restaurant where, as expected, we stopped at two tables on our way to our own so she could show me off to people she knew.

"What did you tell Dad?" I asked.

"Tonight is game one of the NBA finals. You know your father."

I pictured him reclined in his La-Z-Boy, cat perched precariously atop his large belly. Remote in one hand. Beer in the other. Glued to the television. He was not leaving the house for anything.

"I asked around," my mother began. "All of my friends do things alone with their daughters." She said this as if she'd discovered the Mother Lode in her backyard. "In fact, most of them have taken trips together."

It had been years since I'd traveled anywhere with my parents. As schoolteachers, they had the summers off, but more often than not we went to places like Colonial Williamsburg and, once back home, my parents made me written quizzes to confirm I'd learned the appropriate history.

"What did you have in mind?" I leaned back in my chair and picked up my water glass, picturing a nice weekend in Carmel or Napa, sipping wine and reading our books by the pool.

"I want to go to Machu Picchu in early fall."

"Machu Picchu?" I choked on the ice. "That's certainly on my dream destination list."

"I want to hike the Inca trail and spend the night at the ruins." She picked up her fork and dug into her salad.

"What about football season?"

My mother flicked her hand. "They're not supposed to be very good this year."

"You realize this will send Dad over the edge." Whenever my mother and I were out of his sight, my father imagined the worst. As a child I never heard the phrase *go ask your father*; instead my mother constantly overrode him. When he feared my being swept out to sea in the undertow, my mother would tell him to relax. When I climbed trees and he worried I'd fall, my mother just rolled her eyes. I still told him a time half an hour later than I expected to be anywhere to postpone the onset of his anxiety.

My mother bobbed her head and took a sip of wine.

"Let's do it," I said. She was the one who was going to have to deal with him.

"Why did you want to have dinner alone?" my mother asked.

Unwanted tears threatened. I concentrated on stabbing a tomato with my fork without it shooting across the table. My mother remained silent, placing appropriately sized bites of salad in her mouth and dabbing at her lips with her napkin. I set down my silverware.

"Chris and I broke up. I just can't do it anymore. It was supposed to be different when he graduated from the PhD, but nothing has changed."

"We always liked Chris." She gave me a half smile.

"It would be easier if he were a bad person. I've tried to fix it, but I need a partner, not a child."

"I'm glad I have you dear," she covered my hand with hers.

"But no one needs a child."

★ ★ ★

There are only two ways to get to Machu Picchu from the capital city of Cusco: by taking the train along a narrow canyon, then a bus zigzagging up a dirt road cut into the thick jungle, or by hiking the Inca trail. Our journey would take three days on foot from the banks of the muddy Urubamba River in the Sacred Valley of the Gods, to the Sun Gate, the entrance to Machu Picchu. My mother not only wanted to hike, but she also wanted to enjoy herself. The outfitter she picked provided porters to carry all our essentials, tents, food, cookware, and water. All we had to carry were our personal belongings. At first, I felt uncomfortable with the idea of someone else schlepping my gear, but as they unloaded case after case of gourmet food, the benefit became clear. Even though we had enough porters to make an ascent on Everest, this would be no death march.

Our guide was a spry Peruvian named Pedro who had smooth, caramel-colored skin and brown eyes with radiating laugh lines. He had the compact build of a professional soccer player and wore American branded clothing.

"Good morning, my friends," he said throwing his arms wide. "Welcome to my beautiful home. Come sit. I tell you the details of our journey together."

Pedro instructed us to introduce ourselves and tell what we most hoped to experience on our trip. As each group member spoke, my mother took notes. She'd been analyzing the address list since breakfast and was particularly interested in two women who shared our last name.

"Williams is a common name," I said. "Almost as bad as Smith."

"Maybe they're distantly related to us," she said.

Related to *Dad*, I thought.

When it came to my mother's turn, she detailed how she had picked Peru and that this was our first trip together since I'd entered adulthood. She then proceeded to introduce me, talk about my jewelry business, and was starting to explain how I'd moved back to California from Boston, when Pedro and I both cut her off at the same moment.

While the others sorted their gear, and my mother made idle chitchat, I studied the unnecessary trail map—not only was the trail clearly marked by the Inca's stone paving, but our entourage would make it difficult to get lost. Pedro squatted at my side.

"You must select a stone with your left hand," he said in a soft voice. "It is Peruvian belief. You carry stone to the highest point of journey and your wish come true."

"How do you know I have a wish?"

"Pedro see everything." He tapped his index finger next to his eye.

"Then how will I know when we're at the highest point?"

"You will know." Now he thumped his fist twice against his heart. "And Pedro will tell you." He winked.

I scanned the rocks at my feet, turning a few over with the toe of my hiking boot, until I found a flat stone about the size of my thumb and index finger pressed together in the okay sign, perfect for skipping along the surface of a lake. I pocketed it and rubbed my thumb against it, feeling for blemishes.

Once we started hiking, it didn't take long for the group to string out along the trail. The power hikers moved to the front, and the birders drifted to the back, stopping every few feet to peer into the foliage and mark a new species off their life lists. My mother and I floated in the middle.

"It smells just like home," she said. I inhaled. The familiar scent of eucalyptus transported me back to running barefoot all summer with Emily, the medicinal scent of the crushed leaves clinging to our sunburned skin.

★ ★ ★

Emily and I had met for dinner right before I left for Peru. It was rare that she could convince her husband to stay alone with the kids. She was excited to be out.

"Look," she said when we first arrived. "Real napkins. And there are no crayons to color on the tablecloth." After we'd ordered, Emily said, "You need to tell your mother."

I leaned back and took a sip of wine. "What if my mother already knows?"

"Wouldn't she have said something to you?"

The acidity of the wine bit the back of my throat. "Not necessarily," I said. "She's always respected my privacy. She might be waiting for me to come to her."

"This is a pretty big thing to ignore, even for your mother."

"She's just biding her time. Grace Williams has always been skilled at making the best of a situation. She wants everyone to be happy."

"To be happy or appear happy? Your mother can be the queen of denial."

I swirled the wine in my glass. "These days I think of her

more like Lady Justice balancing her scales between me and my father."

"If you say so." Emily sipped her chardonnay. "But we both know you think they tip drastically toward him."

"Remind me why I keep you in my life?"

"Because you love me and I give you such good advice." She blew me a kiss over her wineglass. "Tell your mother."

★ ★ ★

Exhausted when we reached the campsite, my estimation of my mother's intelligence elevated from clever to near genius. While my mother and I relaxed with glasses of white wine and enjoyed the view down to the valley, the porters set up our tents and cooked our four-course dinner. After dinner, we crawled into our tent and settled in for the night. Our rustling sleeping bags, the soft murmur of voices through fabric walls, and the haunting chatter of exotic birds filled the air. When the sun dropped over the horizon, the temperature fell, and the down sleeping bag became a welcome cocoon.

The last time my mother and I had shared a tent was in elementary school on a Girl Scout camping trip. She wasn't my troop leader—that was left to two women who were much artsier and craftier than she was—but she would come along for field trips like horseback riding, visiting the Exploratorium, and seeing the elephant seals during their annual migration at Año Nuevo State Beach. My mother grew up camping with her father, the son of a mill owner in California's Central Valley. Her father spent his childhood exploring the Sierra Nevadas, and family trips always involved a tent. My own father didn't like to be more than a few steps from a flush toilet and a plush bed.

Maybe it was the intimacy of the tent, or the foreign surroundings, or the fact we really were alone together for the first time in years that emboldened me.

"Why do you stay with Dad?" I asked into the darkness. "You can't like his drinking."

She adjusted her pillow. "It's not that I haven't thought about it."

"Really?"

"Well, yes, but look at my friends' husbands. I couldn't deal with John's temper, or how controlling Bob is, or how Scott always has to have the latest gadget and the most expensive car. And forget Tom's Christian fundamentalism."

"But have they fallen out of their chair at the restaurant reaching to place a martini glass back on the table? Do they regularly have to be propped between two people to get across the room? Don't you get tired of always making excuses and having to be the one to drive home?"

"It could be much worse. He doesn't become violent or loud; he's just dopey and maudlin. Really, he's self-medicating to deal with his social anxiety."

"There are drugs for that. Chris was on about ten of them." I studied her shadowy profile. "You love to entertain and he prefers watching sports on TV. You like to travel and go out to dinner. He gets anxious leaving the house."

"But we do travel a lot, and at home he leaves me alone to do the things I want. I play tennis, I read, I volunteer. It's a nice life." She rustled around in her sleeping bag. "I know it's hard for you to understand this, but I fell in love with a different man. To me he's still Richard, and I love him. And anyway, all our friends enjoy a few cocktails. It's generational."

"The only thing generational about alcoholism is that it's hereditary."

"Well then, you can count your blessings that you don't have his genes."

During the worst years of my adolescence, when I couldn't understand why my father wouldn't even try to stop drinking since he seemed so desperate to have a good relationship with me, I held on tightly to being able to distance myself from him because I was adopted. Not being his biological daughter had become as much a part of who I was, or wasn't, as anything else. I couldn't inherit his alcoholism, or his anxiety, or his neediness. While my nature kept the glass half full, his always had a gaping crack in the bottom. All I wanted was for him to put more weight on his relationship with me than on his relationship with alcohol, and to *attempt* to stop drinking, whether that meant rehab or Al-Anon meetings or simply acknowledging his drinking affected our family—and for my mother to stop making it okay for him not to.

★ ★ ★

When I went to college at Amherst, an elite school almost as far away as I could escape while still remaining in the continental US, one of many upsides to my rural isolation was that my parents couldn't drop in unannounced, making college the perfect opportunity to redefine our interaction. If my father wanted to be a part of my life, it would be on my terms. I told my mother in her well-established role of intermediary that I would no longer talk to him unless he admitted he needed help. When my mother requested I phone home every week, I insisted she initiate the calls. She did so every Tuesday, so religiously that my friends knew not to bother trying to reach me during that time window. When my father would inevitably try to sneak onto the second extension, the sound would drop.

"Hello?" I would demand. "Hello?"

"Oh, hello," my father would say, as if caught unaware, even though it happened every week.

"The phone just got real soft. I can't hear."

"Ok, I'll hang up." My father then kept up a steady stream of background dialogue. "Did you tell her about the Jacksons?"

My mother filtered what to pass along, and I developed a minor fascination with the topics he brought up that she chose not to share. I tried not to think about how when we hung up the phone, she would repeat everything I'd said.

★ ★ ★

When I moved back to the Bay Area after eight years of living on the opposite coast, I had mixed feelings about moving home. Although technically following Chris, I was the one returning to family, friends, and a familiar place. My mother and I were on the phone.

"I don't want to see him unless he admits he has a problem," I said.

"He hasn't been so bad lately," she said. "Just give him a chance."

"Mom, you know I can barely be civil to him. You can't like being around me when I'm like that." I paced, my footsteps echoing on the wood floor.

"Well, I'm glad you recognize it, dear."

Chris cursed from the office where he was setting up the computer network in our Southwestern Jail.

"Aren't you sorry you're missing out on a relationship with me?" I asked.

"He's worse around you," she said.

I stopped and took a deep breath. "Because you *are* missing out on it, you know? I shut down around him."

"I think you make him nervous."

"Great, so now it's my fault." I caught sight of my flushed face in the mirror. Turned away. "Can we at least agree that I am not the one with the problem?"

"Just give him a chance."

"Why can't we go out without him?"

"It will upset him."

"Well, it upsets me to have him there."

She sighed. "It's important to me that both of you are there." Perhaps if I had shut her out too, she would have had reason to stop enabling his drinking, but I wanted the same better version of our family that she did. Instead I gave in. For my mother, I made adjustments. We started going out to breakfast because there are only so many alcoholic drinks one can order in the morning.

★ ★ ★

On my last failed attempt to redefine our interaction, I could feel it before I stepped into the house. I'd been putting off having dinner with my parents for several weeks, using a variety of excuses but, in truth, I was spread so thin in my day-to-day life that I needed every minute of peace I could hold onto, and I hated the way I behaved around my father.

"You can't avoid us all summer," my mother had said into the phone. It was true.

While Chris waited in the car, I rang the doorbell and used my key simultaneously, bracing myself. No one came, so I forged ahead down the hallway. The bedroom doorway framed my father's feet resting on the bedspread in mismatched dark socks and brown loafers. He is colorblind, and I used to sort his socks for him so he wouldn't go to work wearing one forest green and the other black.

"Hello?" I said.

"Yoo hoo, we're in here," my mother called from their bathroom.

My father was sprawled on top of the covers, his shirt coming untucked from his waistband, his eyes glassy, his comb-over flopped to the wrong side, exposing a bald head that even he no longer believed he was hiding.

"My knees are bothering me, so I just needed to lie down for a moment," he said as I passed through to find my mother.

I closed the bathroom door behind me. "I see we're off to a good start this evening," I said to my mother. She applied mascara in the mirror.

"I don't know what happened," she said. "I told him not to drink and he said he wasn't, but then I caught him at the garage freezer swigging vodka from the bottle. He knew we were having dinner with you."

"We'll meet you at the restaurant." I walked back down the hallway and out the door without a backward glance.

"That's it. I'm done with this," I said to Chris. "If I didn't think it would break her heart, I wouldn't even go to the restaurant." We sped down the dark roadway. "I don't need this in my life anymore."

"What makes you think you'll be able to stick to it this time?" Chris asked.

I raked my fingers through my hair and let out a long breath. "Wishful thinking."

★ ★ ★

As I lay on my side in the tent next to my mother, I realized there was a question I had never thought to ask her. "Why did you want children?" I said.

My mother sat up and unzipped her duffle bag. "For the usual reasons. To create a family of our own. To raise a child. And it was just what people did." She pulled out her black sleeping mask from the outer pocket and slipped it over her head, but she did not pull it down to cover her eyes. She laid back down on her pillow.

"I'm not sure I was a good mother for you," she said.

"What makes you say that?" I rolled onto my back. I could see stars out the top mesh of our tent.

"You were always so independent. For the most part I just let you be. I could have pushed more. Been more involved."

I laughed. "You were PTA President."

"Not like that," she said. "You were a good kid. You got good grades. You had nice friends. I didn't have to worry about you. Maybe I should have more."

Nocturnal birds called to each other in the jungle around us, filling the silence. I realized I had never wished for a different mother, only that she'd handled my father's alcoholism differently.

"You weren't a bad mother for me. You gave me the space I needed and supported me in everything I did." Someone coughed in the distance. I lowered my voice. "I do wish my father wasn't an alcoholic."

"He loves you," she said.

"That's what makes it so hard."

My mother pulled her black mask down over her eyes. She had slept with the mask for as long as I could remember. Seeing her blindfolded and helpless used to scare me. Anyone could sneak up on her. My father slept with a baseball bat under his side of the bed, but I knew that he would never wake up. It would be up to me to grab the bat and whack an intruder.

★ ★ ★

After a chilly Peruvian night, we woke to a clear morning and began hiking toward Dead Woman's pass, the first of three passes we would climb. I rolled the stone in my pocket. Bromeliads clung to the cliffs, thriving in the moist mountain climate. I couldn't keep an orchid alive at home, even in the bathroom soaking up the steam from the shower, yet here these delicate flowers flourished in the wild. My mother plugged along ahead of me at a steady pace, fit from her weekly tennis game and aerobics classes, pointing out the brightly plumed birds and exotic flowers that caught her eye. I snapped endless photos on my iPhone. When the climb turned strenuous, the group strung out along the trail like breadcrumbs and my mother and I found ourselves hiking alone. She stopped, dug her canteen out of her day pack and took a sip of water. The tooth-like Andes stood sentinel around us.

"I wish your grandfather could see this," she said. My mother offered me the water bottle and I took it. "Speaking of which, your father and I really would like to help you buy a house."

I stopped gulping water and looked at her. She wore sturdy light-hiking boots, multipocketed trekking pants that zipped off to form shorts, and carried a light backpack that held water, a camera, and a pair of binoculars. A color-coordinated bandana hung around her neck, and she had traded her oversized Jackie O sunglasses for a sportier version.

"You don't have to do that."

"Our parents helped us. You're an only child. Eventually it will be your money. We would rather you enjoy it while we're still around to see it."

I screwed the cap back on the water bottle and returned it to her. I pictured the stonewall-lined driveway and the Adirondack chairs beckoning from the farmhouse porch.

"Thank you, but it's not about the money. A house is a big commitment. I don't want to go into it lightly."

"I thought you wanted to stay in the Bay Area now that you're not tied to Chris."

"I do. But I've also been missing New England lately." I studied her for a reaction. She replaced the water bottle in her backpack and resumed hiking up the trail.

We wound between two lakes and soon the pass where Pedro waited appeared. As we neared the summit, I smoothed my fingers over my stone, still memorizing each flaw on its surface.

"Here?" I asked Pedro, tensing.

He shook his head. "This is false summit."

We hiked through an ancient tunnel cut into the mountain. My mother's head bent to watch her foot placement. The forest formed a leafy cathedral over us, and heavy mist obscured the view as if we inhabited the clouds themselves.

"Is this about Chris?" my mother asked. Mud sucked at our boots, and water seeped into the empty footprints behind us. "You were with him a long time. Maybe you imagined buying a house together, and it doesn't seem right to do it alone."

I halted briefly. "This has nothing to do with Chris."

We emerged from the wet cotton ball into bright sunshine. Jagged peaks surrounded us and we could see down two separate river valleys.

"Just remember," my mother said. "The longer you wait, the higher the price will be."

I stiffened, suspecting she was talking about more than just real estate. My wish solidified.

★ ★ ★

As we neared the next summit, I smoothed my fingers over my stone's now familiar flaws.

"We are here." Pedro nodded to me after we crested the pass. "The highest point of our journey."

Pedro had said I needed to place the stone with my right hand for my wish to come true. I glanced around for a spot where it would stay put. Two large boulders stacked on the summit created a safe cavity between them. Rubbing the stone's surface as if the rock were a genie's bottle I concentrated on my wish, then I set it in its new resting place. The Incan Gods now held my fate.

When I returned, Pedro said, "Don't be fooled. We still have long journey from here."

"You're telling me," I said.

★ ★ ★

We reached the Sun Gate the next afternoon, and I looked down on Machu Picchu for the first time. It seemed impossible.

Lines of silver stones formed intricate patterns against the bright green grass, like an ancient labyrinth cradled in the palm of a mountaintop, protected by jagged peaks. A road corkscrewed its way through the jungle from the valley below. A photo would not do the view justice, but I took fifteen shots anyway. The thought that we were going closer, down into the heart of the ruins, kept me still.

"Isn't that incredible?" my mother said from my shoulder. I startled, caught in the view I only dreamed of seeing when I came across it in adventure magazines, but here I was thanks to her.

"Impossible."

"Shall we?" She started off down the stone-lined trail.

I put my iPhone in my pocket and stepped from the platform of the Sun Gate. The trail clung to the sweep of the mountainside, the view of Machu Picchu disappearing and reappearing as the dense vegetation played a frustrating game of peekaboo. Each time the jungle let us view the ruins, I snapped a picture of what I knew was as impossible to catch as a person's soul. As we moved closer, the walls of intricately locked stones came into focus, and the multicolored dots materialized into visitors. Alpacas lumbered from one terrace to the next, grazing on the new green grass between the ruins. The late-afternoon sun slanted through the clouds below us and illuminated the lower side, as if highlighted by the Incan Gods.

Our group tightened around Pedro like the eager Peruvian children who followed us in town, as he explained the history and intrigue of each hidden chamber. The elaborate levees built to channel water throughout the city still flowed. An accurate sundial marked time in the same increments we use today. And on the solstice, the sun would shine perfectly through the center of a tiny opening. It was hard for me to imagine how such an emerging society could not only get the stone to the top of the mountain, but cut it so perfectly that it fit together, not a hair's width apart, centuries later.

In the far corner of the citadel, a flat slab of granite stood alone like a backdrop to an open dirt stage. A woman in Levi's stood facing it, arms stretched and held inches away from the rock as if someone had a gun to her back and she was forbidden to touch the surface. Her head was turned and her eyes were closed.

"What do you think she's doing?" I asked my mother.

"Some people feel an energy coming off the rock," she whispered back.

I raised my eyebrows. "Are you sure that's not just radiant heat from the sun that's been shining on it all day?"

"That might be the practical explanation for it, dear, but some people like to believe there are forces bigger than themselves."

"Are you suggesting a higher power?" I clasped my hand to heart in mock surprise.

She put her hands on her hips. "I'm suggesting that there doesn't have to be a logical explanation. Some things you might just want to take on faith."

"Is this going to turn into a 'God has a higher plan for us' lecture, because you know I don't believe in all that."

"Sometimes in our lives we are given gifts, whether or not we recognize them as such at the time," she said. "I just hope that you are not so busy being practical that you miss those gifts."

I fiddled with my necklace. The woman dropped her arms to her sides and stepped back from the slab with a moist look in her eyes.

"You want to try it?" My mother nodded to the rock.

"Why not?" I shrugged. We both stepped forward and assumed the gunpoint position. I kept my fingers an inch from the stone like the woman, waiting for electricity to jump from the granite into my fingers. I closed my eyes and concentrated. Was that something? I pressed my hands to the stone. It was slightly warm to the touch.

"Did you feel anything?" I asked.

"An inner sense of calm," my mother said. "And you?"

"A rock that's been warmed by the sun."

★ ★ ★

The crowds thinned, leaving with the last train to Cusco. Our accommodations for the night were in the only hotel on the mountain. A four-star blot on the landscape I would have protested were I not about to reap the benefits. When searching for an outfitter, another criterion we agreed on was visiting the ruins by moonlight. After hot showers and a buffet dinner of traditional Peruvian fare—ceviche, alpaca, and twenty kinds of potatoes—Pedro gathered us.

"This is a very, very special place." He stretched his arms to embrace Machu Picchu. "And I am very happy to share it with you, my friends."

My mother and I claimed a large rock that perched above the cradle of the valley and watched the ruins come to life in the moonlight—as if the rocks themselves captured the beams and threw them back up into the heavens, glowing with a life of their own. The sky was filled with pricks of light, and the surrounding peaks of the Andes protected us.

"There's something about this place," I whispered to my mother. "I don't know if it's an energy, or if it's just too hard for me to comprehend how they built this so long ago in such an impossible location, but I definitely feel something, like all my senses are working at their highest setting."

"It's remarkable, isn't it?"

"And to think, even after all this time, no one knows for sure why it was built or why it was abandoned."

"One of the great mysteries of the world."

"How could they leave such a place? They had everything they needed—running water, a defendable perimeter, a road, a view . . ."

"I'm sure there was a very good reason," said my mother.

"But if it was a good reason, don't you think someone would have figured it out by now? What if the King just decided he wanted something different, and no one challenged him?"

"We can't suppose to know the concerns they were facing at the time."

"What could have been so bad to abandon this entire city?" I opened my arms like Pedro, embracing the ruins.

"If a decision needed to be made quickly, it might not have been fully thought out."

Mine was a closed adoption. We knew no details beyond what was in that file folder. But now a door had opened. "Are we still talking about Machu Picchu?" I asked.

"You tell me, dear."

I smoothed my hands over the slab we sat on, feeling all its rough bumps and nicks, like I had with the stone in my pocket. I pictured my rock secure between the two boulders. The Incan Gods sitting on a panel deciding how to honor my wish. By now our eyes had adjusted to the moonlight. The ruins were almost as visible as they had been during the day, although with softened edges. Machu Picchu spread before us. Somehow, the same moonlight that shone on the farmhouse in Maine and the cottage with the red door in California infused the ruins with a mystical power.

"Mom," I turned away from the citadel to face her. "The reason I'm hesitating on buying a house is because—as improbable as it seems—my birth mother died recently and left me her house in Maine."

My mother gasped. "She died? When?"

"When you were on the Rhine."

Her brow furrowed. "But that was last month."

"I'm sorry. I should have told you."

My mother put her hand on my shoulder, squeezed, then looked up to the stars. She was silent. Contemplative. Her thoughts unreadable to me.

"There's something I need to tell you too." My mother turned to face me. "Your father and I bought the house Eileen showed you. The one with the studio out back." She shook her head. "It fit you so perfectly, we didn't want you to miss the opportunity."

I sat up straight and slapped my hands to my thighs. "What? You did not!"

"We thought it would be a good investment, even if you didn't want it. It's in the perfect neighborhood for a rental, as you well know."

Even when we think we're prepared, earthquakes always hit when we least expect them.

CHAPTER ELEVEN

Lindsay

The taillights of the airport shuttle glowed red at the end of the driveway when the driver braked before turning back onto the main road. My luggage, piled next to one of the Adirondack chairs, contained everything I needed for an indeterminate stay. In the garden, the plants were engaged in a war to choke each other off from the nutrients of the sun, reminding me of a Rousseau painting. I half expected a monkey to poke his face out of the leaves.

Beverly may have let the garden return to a primal state, but she kept the house spotless. She'd left a note saying "Welcome home" propped against a vase of fresh flowers on the kitchen island. I flipped the card facedown on the counter.

My stomach felt a little queasy, I assumed from something I ate on the plane. Walking room-to-room, I opened windows to stir the stale air. The house still had a museum-like quality, but now it felt more similar to the first day we opened the cabin we rented every summer in the Sierras. Familiar yet foreign. Clean yet musty. Me anxious to start a summer of hiking and waterskiing.

The family whose private art collection I managed had always allowed me flexibility, and aside from occasionally needing to be onsite to oversee shipments and inventory I worked remotely. It had been easy to sublet the Southwestern Jail to two graduate students who welcomed its proximity to the university. Even easier to tell people I needed a change of scenery. I posted a picture of Tahoe on my Facebook page and left it at that.

By the time I opened all the windows and brought my luggage inside, the sun had begun to set. Although exhausted, I wouldn't be able to sleep until I set up my jewelry studio. Upstairs, neither guest room had a good flat work surface. Downstairs, not ready to encroach on Claire's memorabilia-filled work space, I sealed off her office. My stomach settled as soon as the lock clicked into place.

The air in the dining room felt less likely to spontaneously combust. It opened to the main room with a set of French doors and was comfortable, yet impersonal, with good light from the windows and a large table. I found a washable, striped, sage tablecloth in the buffet and had spread it across the oak table, before it occurred to me that I owned both the table and the cloth. If I damaged the surface, I was the only one who would care.

I admired the sophisticated white dishes artfully stacked in the glass-faced cabinet. A smile tugged at the corner of my mouth. The dishes were mine too. So was the buffet. I unpacked my jewelry-making supplies—the beads, the wire, my tools for bending the metal into the shapes I desired—and arranged them across the table in their familiar places. I ate my bag of airplane pretzels for dinner and went up to bed early. Before turning off the light, I cleared the picture frames off the dresser, shoving them inside a drawer that I yanked open and shut as if it housed a gremlin trying to escape. But I left out the jewelry box.

★ ★ ★

The doorbell chimed and I rolled over in bed. It was already eight in the morning, but with the time change I felt drugged.

It rang again, and I reached deep within my body and willed myself to get up. Nothing happened.

"Lindsay?" a low voice called out. "I'm letting myself in." Toenails clicked on the wood floors, and I heard a jingle of tags. I opened one eye. The dog ran up the stairs, crossed the bedroom, and landed on the mattress with a lightness that belied his eighty pounds. He started licking my face, and I mumbled "no kisses" before throwing up my arm in defense. The dog stood over me and bounced the bed. I groaned and sat up. He jumped down and took a few steps to the door, looking back over his shoulder. Willing me to follow.

I pushed the covers aside, pulled my hair into a ponytail, and trailed him downstairs in my pajamas and bare feet. Halfway down, my foot hovered above the next step and I smoothed my hair. Most of it seemed to be caught in the hastily wrapped ponytail band. I checked myself quickly in the mirror in the entry hall.

Lucas busied himself brewing coffee in the kitchen. He'd even brought milk.

"Bless you," I said when he handed me a mug, *my mug*.

"Not a morning person, huh?"

I shook my head, still sipping my coffee, and appraised him over the rim. I should have showered.

"I'm headed to work, so I thought I'd drop off Riley."

"Thank you." The caffeine began to take effect. "Thank you for everything."

"It's good to have you back." He smiled. I smiled back. We both focused on our coffee cups. "Well, I have to get going," Lucas said, checking the time on his phone and taking one last sip. "You two have fun together today."

"Thanks." I smiled dumbly again.

He set his mug next to *my* sink, and started to the door. The dog looked from him, to me, and back to him again with one ear cocked. "You're staying here boy," Lucas said.

The two of us stood framed in the doorway like a pair of orphans, watching Lucas climb into his truck. The dog whined softly.

"I know how you feel," I said. The dog thumped his tail on the ground. When I looked down at him, he lifted his pleading eyes to mine.

"Wait," I yelled to Lucas. "How about I make you dinner tonight?" I paused. "And Beverly too."

"Sounds good."

"Okay, see you at sixish then." Lucas waved and pulled down the driveway.

"Crap," I said to the dog. "Now what am I going to cook?"

★ ★ ★

After Lucas left, the dog and I climbed back in bed. "This is now my bed," I said running my hands along the smooth, coffee-colored headboard carved into a sleigh. The dog narrowed his eyes at me. "Fine. Our bed. Happy?"

We slept well into midmorning, emerging into the full light of a crisp New England day. The air had a sharp, dry feeling, like everything had just come more fully into focus against the sky-blue backdrop. The yellow of the ragweed more golden. The white of the church steeple just a little cleaner. The green rolling hills more vibrant than before. Out the dormer window, the giant beech tree's leaves had just started to turn in preparation for the long winter ahead.

I pulled on jeans and a sweatshirt. After pouring myself another cup of coffee, I roamed the house in the fresh light. My tools waited in their places on the table, yet my fingers didn't itch to roll the beads between them and feel the surface flaws. I rearranged the tools, appreciating the weight of each in my hands as I moved the small bent-nose pliers, the wire cutter, and the hand drill around on the table as if trying to solve a jigsaw puzzle.

Opening the cases of semi-precious stones, I tried to imagine what design would be ideal for each, my standard trick when I wasn't feeling engaged, but images of my mother Claire, Beverly, and Lucas swirled through my head. I snapped the cases shut.

In the living room, I stood with my hands on my hips in front of the looming stone fireplace, hoping it wouldn't come to life and swallow me. I touched the book spines, lying to myself it was just like browsing a public library. The books were alphabetized and organized in sections—fiction, travel, garden, and history—similar to mine. My parents' bookshelves were arranged by size and color, which was aesthetically pleasing but unhelpful when you actually wanted to find something. I couldn't bring myself to pull a book out and read pages she had read. Photographs lined the shelves, and Claire's stare burned between my shoulder blades like a painting whose eyes follow you to every corner of the room. I grabbed one of the empty boxes that had stored my jewelry supplies, swept all the pictures and personal knickknacks into the box, shut them in the office, then wiped my hands on my jeans.

The kitchen had Claire's touch too. Her cards magnetized to the refrigerator door. Her gleaming pots and pans. The high-end appliances she selected. But it still looked staged for a photo you'd see in a lifestyle magazine, not like a kitchen that regular people owned and used. After clearing the front of the refrigerator of everything but the Robert Frost poem and pouring myself a third cup of coffee, I sat on the front porch in the Adirondack chair, my legs curled beneath me. Everything from here to the road was mine—the beech tree, the stone wall, the driveway. The dog lay with his front paws crossed, surveying the front yard as if lord of the kingdom.

"Come on." I unfolded my legs. "Let's go see if we can find Beverly's house and invite her for dinner."

The dog sprang from the porch and headed past the fenced garden. A pathway cut through the trees in the direction Beverly had indicated, and white shingles peeked through the leaves. I strolled, smelling the damp earthy air, listening to the buzz of insects, and memorizing the details of the landscape—the tiger lilies, the ragweed, the Queen Anne's lace, and the curve of the stone wall. I picked a dandelion and blew the fluffy white seeds so they flew like tiny helicopters scattering on the breeze. Fallen leaves padded the ground and absorbed my footsteps.

The dog was sitting at the side door. Music, the light folksy stuff you hear at a coffee shop, drifted from within the house. My jewelry pieces were often inspired by the melody of background music. I knocked loudly. It seemed awkward to be arriving at the side door, but Riley had not led me astray so far.

"I was hoping you'd be by today!" Beverly exclaimed, opening the door and hugging me in one grand motion. The smell of frying bacon wafted out, and the dog rushed past her into the house. "Come in. Have you had lunch?"

"I hate to admit I've just woken up."

"That's nothing to be ashamed of. I was just starting to make myself a BLT. Can I make you one too?"

My manners told me to say no, but the bacon smell curled around my nose and I had no real food in the house. "That'd be great." I sat in a kitchen chair and watched her assemble the sandwiches. The dog looked hopeful.

"This is just what Claire and I used to do," Beverly said. Her eyes looked glassy. "I do miss her."

I nodded and tightened my grip on my napkin.

"How was Peru?"

"It was amazing." I detailed the trip, focusing on the sites and the food, carefully picking my words as if doing the *New York Times* crossword puzzle in pen to avoid talk of my mother.

"Do you travel much?"

"Are you familiar with Beyond Borders?"

I made motions like I didn't want to talk with my mouth full and imagined my mother detailing my life to Claire and Beverly as they rode camels across the Sahara, then made an elaborate show of swallowing. The dog nudged my hand, placing his head underneath my palm. I slowly stroked between his kind, chocolate eyes. He looked content. Maybe Claire was right to leave him with me.

"Actually, my parents travel with them a lot." I looked up from Riley to Beverly. "They're big fans."

"I see." She frowned.

Arranging my face into a smile, I said, "The main reason I stopped by was to see if you wanted to come for dinner tonight with Lucas. As a thank you." Beverly's smile returned, and she accepted my invitation and provided advice on the nearest grocery store. Riley inhaled his BLT.

★ ★ ★

I pulled all the cookbooks off the shelf and fanned them across the counter, cursing myself for inviting not one, but two, people to dinner. Poisoning them would mean a poor start to my social life in Maine. If I measured ingredients exactly, leveling off tablespoons and squatting down to counter level to squint at the lines on the side of the measuring cup, and if I measured time to the nearest one hundredth of a second, recipes came out tasting right, but if I deviated, or God forbid, improvised a meal, all bets were off. Cooking shows fascinated me. I couldn't fathom how people knew what spices a dish needed just by tasting it. The celebrity chefs who could create elaborate five-course meals out of the same obscure secret ingredient in just one hour dumbfounded me.

I flipped through the cookbooks looking for a recipe that didn't have a list of ingredients filling the page. *The Silver Palate* had good basic recipes and an East Coast flare. All my cookbooks came from restaurants in the Napa Valley and featured

California cuisine. Beverly, and especially Lucas, did not strike me as the artichoke-and-avocado type, and in the land of lobster you'd be hard pressed to find Dungeness crab. I settled on Chicken Dijonnaise, rosemary roasted red potatoes, and creamed spinach, plain enough for the puritans, but still satisfying to the Californian. The chicken recipe came from *The Silver Palette*, and the potatoes were simple enough that I'd memorized the recipe (red potatoes, olive oil, garlic, and rosemary mixed together and baked) and served it to all my California friends who still ate carbs. The spinach was my mother's classic, one box of frozen chopped spinach and half a can of Campbell's Cream of Mushroom soup, which was not so much cooking as reheating and summed up the food I ate as a child. I had tried alternate recipes from scratch, but none tasted right. I knew better than to mess with a good thing.

Shopping list in hand, I had pulled my keys from my purse before I realized I didn't have my car, and Claire's had been totaled in the accident. I froze, took a deep breath, found a key hanging on a hook by the door, and strode to the garage. The truck listed in her assets turned out to be a ten-year-old Pathfinder that made strange rattling noises and listed to the left. At fifty miles an hour the steering wheel shook, but it evened out five miles per hour in either direction. Black dog hair matted the carpets and seats, and one passenger window didn't roll down. It was a manual transmission, four-wheel drive, V6 engine with a trailer hitch. The front windshield had strange oval marks on it that I couldn't figure out, until Riley jumped from the cargo area, crossed the back seat, stepped over the gear box, and sat in the front passenger seat pressing his nose against the glass— the true owner of the truck made apparent. I rolled down the passenger window and he stuck out his head, ears flapping in the breeze.

I found the store and returned safely with the ingredients. In the living room, I risked opening a cabinet to find the stereo and dismissed it as luck when I located it on the first try. I connected my phone, punched the button that said "kitchen speakers," and my familiar boy-band playlist blasted through the house. Now I felt ready to cook. Compared to the broom-closet-sized space in the Southwestern Jail where I couldn't take two steps without knocking my knee against a major appliance, this kitchen was a dream.

Riley kept himself immediately under foot, following me back and forth between the fridge and the counter until I tripped on him, nearly dropping the raw chicken on the floor.

"This is not going to work," I said. "You already had a BLT." I walked forward, pushing him back like a lineman holding the offense at bay while the quarterback scrambled to throw a Hail Mary. Once we reached the other side of the island, I drew an imaginary line with my toe between us on the tile floor.

"You are not to cross this line until I say so." Riley groaned and slumped down with his chin resting on his paws.

I placed the *Silver Palate* opened to Chicken Dijonnaise in the cookbook holder. I usually tried to press the pages flat by resting one of the ingredients on the book, but that inevitably led to food-splattered and stuck-together recipes. The holder solved that problem. The baking dishes were stored right where they should be, next to the gas range oven, and the mixing bowls lived under the mixer in the first cabinet I opened. I needed a slotted spoon and instinctively reached for a large drawer on my left, and there it was. The hairs on the back of my neck stood. I poured a goblet's worth of wine.

I cooked as if being guided by a more experienced hand. I imagined growing up with a mother who taught me to make recipes handed down from generations of my blood relations. We'd have our traditional family meal for each holiday. It would be a rite of passage the first time I was allowed to bake great-grandma's cherry bundt cake with the secret splash of rum. I was visualizing presenting the cake to my real family when I burned my knuckle on the rack putting the chicken and potatoes into the oven. I stuck it into my mouth and scrambled to the sink to run my hand under cool water.

After the initial bite eased, I sat at the stool and tried to sip my wine. My hands shook. I gripped the glass tighter, threatening the delicate stem. Hot tears rolled down my cheeks against my will. I dried my eyes on the corner of my apron and took a deep breath. Beverly and Lucas were almost due.

★ ★ ★

Beverly stood in the living room looking at the shelves. "You've moved things."

"Yes, I set up my jewelry studio in the dining room. I thought we could eat outside."

Lucas walked into the dining room and picked up one of my necklaces.

"I meant the pictures." Beverly moved toward the office. I stepped between her and the door.

"I've been meaning to ask you," I said. "Claire had some of my jewelry designs. Do you know how she got them?"

"I like this red one," Lucas called. "Is it a garnet?"

"Your jewelry?" Beverly asked.

"Tourmaline," I said. "It's actually native to Maine."

"You must be mistaken." Beverly took a sip of her wine.

"That's what I thought." I crossed my arms on my chest. "But I recognize my own work."

"No," she shook her head.

I tucked a loose piece of hair behind my ear. "Claire never said anything to you about how she got them?" Beverly's eyes narrowed. I walked to the bookshelf and trailed my finger across the spines, pausing at Jane Austen, then turned to look back at her.

"Did she mention me by chance?"

Beverly started nodding and her hair bounced. "Claire was my best friend." She kept nodding like a bobble doll. "We shared everything."

"More wine?" Lucas hovered with the bottle. My glass was still full and Beverly held hers between us like a chardonnay shield.

I took a deep sip. "Anyway, I was just wondering."

"I did notice you're wearing her favorite bracelet." Beverly reached out, took my wrist and lifted it under my nose. Riley sat on my foot and looked up at us.

"I like that bracelet," Lucas said.

"Thank you." I stared at Beverly. "I made it."

"You're mistaken." She dropped my wrist. Riley licked my palm.

I sighed. "I wish I was. Dinner?" I impersonated my mother with the brightness of my tone.

"I'm starving," said Lucas.

Dinner turned out better than I expected, and I rated Chicken Dijonnaise a check plus. Fireflies blinked in the dusk, and we kept the mosquitoes at bay with citronella candles. I had to put on a wool coat, while Beverly and Lucas laughed at my thin California blood. Riley lay under the table, stretched so that he touched all three pairs of feet. After Lucas updated Beverly on his mother, who apparently owned the bookstore in town, and Beverly talked about her upcoming trip to Boston to see her family, I asked Beverly how she met Claire.

"Fate brought her to me when she bought the house next door," she said. "Claire was barely older than you, but she'd had more than her fair share of tragedy. She lost her parents when she was young, and then her husband died."

The world seemed to slant for a moment. I pressed my toes into Riley's warm fur to ground myself. Lucas topped off my wine.

"She wanted to put all that sadness behind her. I had just gotten divorced and we became fast friends. I don't know who needed who more. We were there for each other and shared everything. Boy, do I miss her." Beverly dabbed her napkin into the corner of her eye. "But now I've been blessed with the next best thing, her daughter." She clasped her hands together in front of her on the table and smiled.

I gripped the back of my neck, twisting it. "How did they die?"

"Oh," Beverly covered her mouth. "Forgive me. Her parents," she hesitated. "Your grandparents died in a plane crash, and Claire's husband had Hodgkin's disease."

I pressed my lips together.

"That was a lovely dinner," Beverly said quickly. "You obviously have your mother's talent in the kitchen."

"Oh I hope not, my mother's a disaster."

"I meant Claire."

I did my best not to react.

"Can I help you clean up?" Lucas stood and picked up my plate. Riley popped out from under the table.

"Yes," I said. "Thank you."

Beverly made an excuse about needing her beauty sleep, thanked me, and left.

"Now that Beverly's gone, do you want me to help you move any of the larger pieces of furniture?" Lucas winked at me.

"Was it bad to move things?"

He shrugged. "It's your house. Do whatever you want."

"Something feels off. I'm not sure Beverly knew about me. Did you know about me before Claire died?"

"No, but why would I? Claire was my mom's friend."

"Good point." Riley was sacked out in his plaid bed next to the fireplace trying to watch us, but his eyes kept drooping shut. "How about I build a fire and you open another bottle of wine?" I said.

"Don't you want *me* to build the fire while *you* open the wine?"

"I was a Girl Scout."

"Who do you think split those logs outside?"

"Tomorrow you can show me how."

When Lucas returned with the wine, I'd lost myself staring into the flames.

"Why do I feel such loss over people I never thought about before now?"

Riley stood up, stretched into Downward Dog and then trotted over and hopped on the couch between us. He put his head in my lap and pressed his feet against Lucas's legs, separating us. I stroked his silky black ear. Lucas draped his arm across the back of the couch, his fingers resting lightly on the leather behind my head. "It's a strange situation, but I admire that you're here. It's very bold."

"Bold? Ha. Clearly you don't know me very well."

He smiled at me. "I hope to change that."

Lucas stayed until we'd finished a second bottle and let the fire burn itself down to glowing embers, Riley between us like a chaperone with a ruler at a Junior High School dance.

★ ★ ★

I woke with a headache. The kibble Riley inhaled for breakfast rattled against the side of his bowl and echoed between my ears. I filled a Nalgene bottle with water and took a gulp, steadying myself against the sink, then wiped my mouth on the back of my sleeve. Bold. I didn't feel bold. When my father's anxiety overtook him, he became frenetic, pacing, cursing, ricocheting from perceived fear to perceived fear in a jumble of words and movement. As a child I would watch my mother to gauge the proper DEFCON level, but she always remained unruffled as he barked orders that she dismissed with a shake of her head.

Without missing a beat, she would mark her page in her book, or place her tea on the coaster, or stop matching socks fresh from the drier, and resolve the issue before returning to her previous activity. I'd been raised to be practical.

"Come on," I said, and Riley trotted after me down to the dock. Earlier, I'd found a canoe in the garage. Now I wrestled it off its cart and into the water. The words *Old Town* were painted in white on the green fiberglass hull. Riley hopped in the center and I climbed into the back. Over the side, all I saw was my serious reflection framed by the trees behind me. I stuck out my tongue.

I stroked toward the center of the lake, the smooth and flat surface making it easy to skate across its plane. Trees crowded along the shore, and the water reflected each leaf like a mirror. There was hardly any breeze. The water drops from the dip of my paddle pattered on the lake surface. Dragonflies flitted alongside my canoe, occasionally landing on the frame to catch a brief ride. When I reached the spot, I stopped paddling and looked over the side.

Ghostlike bleached arms of felled trees reached up for me through the murky water like the kelp forests in California. As a child I hated the feel of seaweed wrapping around my body when I swam in the ocean. I would panic and splash as if it were a live monster from the deep trying to drag me under to my death. Just the lightest touch of the tentacle would send me sprinting to shore. Nothing ever happened, but my fear of the unknown was instinctual.

The stump pathway led me to the middle of the lake, where I searched under the water for remnants of the sunken town. Riley stood on the canoe's front seat and stared over the bow as if wondering what I was looking for. No houses. No streets. No church steeples. Just murky green water reflecting the sun. While I was imagining the houses drowned and furniture struggling to escape out the windows, the canoe dipped and Riley launched himself into the lake with a splash. I dropped the paddle in the bottom and grasped the sides.

"Get back in the boat!" He cocked his head and lapped water with his tongue as if to prove to me it was safe. I grabbed for his collar. The canoe lurched. He dodged my reach like a pro running back.

I pressed my fingers to my temples and watched him swim, his tail wagging in the water. When Riley paddled within reach, I braced my knees wide against the bottom of the canoe, grabbed his collar with my right hand and the base of his tail with my left, then threw myself backward, hoping to use my body weight to drag him in the boat on top of me. The side dipped low. Water rushed over the edge. And I somersaulted over Riley into the lake.

A blanket of water poured over my head and into my ears and nose. Thrashing about, I searched for the surface. The vast emptiness of the lake expanded in all directions. No kelp, or fish, or lake bottom to ground me. Just plankton suspended in the water. Somewhere below me, a decaying town. Above me, a serene day on the lake.

The longer I indulged my anxiety, the more danger I would be in. As a form of rebellion, or perhaps to prove a point, I had learned to control my nerves. Something else my father could never be bothered to attempt. Now I stilled myself, utilized my SCUBA training to note which direction my bubbles were floating, and followed their trajectory as my visual lifeline to the surface. Directly overhead I saw the canoe bottom. Riley's legs and underbelly pranced in circles a few feet away. I swam to them.

When my head broke the surface, I inhaled a gasp of air. Bicycling my legs to keep afloat and ward off evils rising from the depths, I took quick breaths. My eyes darted to the shore. A good long swim away. I hooked my elbows over the edge of the canoe and tried to heave myself in, but the side dipped under my weight, and I slipped back into the water. The boat righted itself. I tried again, kicking my feet for upward motion, but the lake dragged me back down.

Without putting my face in the water, like my mother when she doesn't want to get her hair wet, I swam for the shore, tugging the canoe behind me by its rope. After five hundred yards, I clung to the side, sputtering, trying to catch my breath. Riley doggie-paddled next to me, lapping a few more sips of lake water.

Each stroke took me farther from the sunken town and closer to solid ground. When my feet touched the rocky shore, I hoisted myself onto dry land and lay face up, staring at the sharp blue sky, panting. An eagle flew overhead. Riley threaded himself over the rocks and shook. Lake water flew everywhere. He sat next to me and licked my cheek. I dug my fingers into his wet coat and lay still until my breathing eased.

CHAPTER TWELVE

Lindsay

The words *Pen & Ink* were painted in black script on the bookstore window. Outside the door sat a bench with a stainless-steel dog dish beneath a water spigot. I smiled, imagining Riley drinking his fill. When I pushed open the door, a bell jingled. The bookstore had hardwood floors, plenty of thick throw rugs, and bookshelves from floor to ceiling that created nooks and crannies with armchairs that invited customers to sit and read the afternoon away. It smelled like clean paper, coffee, and a hint of vanilla. I might never leave.

A few other customers browsed the shelves. I ordered a latte from a college-age guy with tattoos at the small espresso counter in the front corner. Coffee in hand, I scanned the titles, stopping every so often to pick up a book and read the blurbs on the back. No one paid me any attention. A woman with a pen tucked behind her ear sat at the bookstore register chewing on a No. 2 pencil and scribbling notes in a small spiral binder. She had Lucas's coloring and wore glasses. I swallowed. When I approached her, she glanced up and gave me a quizzical look.

"Have we met?" Her voice had the same musical tones as her son's.

I hesitated. "I'm Lindsay Williams?" My voice raised in a question mark. "Claire's daughter?"

"It's you," she whispered, dropping her notebook on the counter and coming around the side to see me. "I'm so sorry I haven't made it out to the house yet. It's been crazy here. We've been taking inventory." She ran her fingers through her blond hair, sounding as nervous as I felt. "I'm Lauren." She held out her hand, which I shook.

"Claire was my best friend. I miss her terribly." She signaled to the guy working the espresso bar to cover the register, then led me to a small patio off the back of the store. We settled into two cushioned chairs facing each other, separated by a small table. Several large potted plants decorated the patio, and a hummingbird feeder hung from a trellis.

"So, how's everything going?" Lauren asked.

I hesitated. Maybe it was a resemblance to Lucas. Maybe it was just her empathy. But something about her put me at ease.

"It's all just been a little overwhelming, to tell you the truth."

"I can't imagine." She reached out and touched my arm. "I'm sorry." She squeezed. "I really should have come out there, but I wasn't sure I could handle it or what I'd even say to you."

"So you and Claire were close."

Lauren looked at me over her glasses. "Very. I knew Claire in college."

"In California?"

She bit her lower lip. "Actually, here in town. Godfrey. Our schools had an exchange program. She came here her junior year."

"Is that how you both ended up in Babcock Falls?"

"I met my husband in grad school in Boston, and he was offered a tenured position at Godfrey over twenty years ago, so we moved up here then. Claire moved here when her husband died. I don't think she knew where else to go. She always had a special draw to Lone Loon Pond." Lauren cast her eyes down for a moment and then looked back up at me, as if she'd made a decision. "You never searched for her?"

Over her shoulder a hummingbird hovered at the feeder, its wings a blur as it inserted its razorlike beak into the drinking spout. A squirrel ran across the top of the trellis, reminding me of my mother's never-ending quest to protect her bird feeder from the bushy-tailed thugs.

"No," I said. "And now," I sucked in my cheeks, "I'm living in her house, caring for her dog, meeting her friends, but I just can't wrap my head around the concept that there are people who share my genes."

I stood, walked over to one of the terra-cotta pots and rubbed the leaves of a lavender plant, releasing its scent. "My life wasn't perfect, but I was loved unconditionally."

"I think Claire would appreciate that."

"Shouldn't she have left the house to someone else?"

"If her husband had lived long enough for them to start a family, I don't think any of this would have happened. She wouldn't have even been in Maine. It took her profound grief over his death to bring her back here."

I rubbed my face with my hands. "So neither of us would have chosen this."

"No. But what you decide to do now is your choice." She stared at me, then shook her head. "Your resemblance to Claire is kind of disturbing." Lauren dropped her head back against the chair cushion, staring into the sky. "When I think of Claire, I picture her now, but seeing you brings me right back to senior year at Godfrey." She looked at me again. "God, we were so young."

"I'm sorry," I said. "It must be awful for you to have her gone so unexpectedly. Lucas said she was family."

Lauren's eyes filled with tears. "Thank you. Yes," she said.

"I'm still in shock. When Lucas told me he met you, all I wanted to do was call Claire and plot how we would get you two together so that we could share grandchildren." She laughed, dabbing her eyes. "No pressure, of course."

"On that note," I said, blushing, "I'll let you get back to your customers."

"Lindsay," she stopped me.

"Yes."

"It's really nice to meet you. I'm sorry that Claire never got the chance."

"Thank you," I said. "It's nice to meet you too." I started to leave and then turned back.

"I hope that I will get to know Claire through you."

She nodded, then bit her lip again. "I'd like that."

★ ★ ★

After returning home from the bookstore, I laced up my hiking boots, draped Riley's leash around my neck, filled my water bottle, and stepped out the back door. I always think better when I'm moving, and something nagged from the corner of my mind. The crisp fall day reminded me of sitting in the stands at Amherst College, sipping from a thermos filled with hot apple cider, and watching a football game on par with my high school team. Riley trotted ahead, stopping to smell each leaf, flower, and twig that caught his attention. Some items warranted intense scrutiny, while others were passed by with only a cursory sniff and a lifted leg.

We started along the lakeside path in a clockwise direction from the farmhouse. I had barely explored the area and was happy to see a worn trail in the direction I wanted to hike. The path meandered along the lakeshore, over exposed roots, rocks, and bare ground, and soon came to a carved wooden sign where another trail forked to the left. According to the marker, we could continue around the lake or take the spur trail 2.5 miles to the top of Mount Bascom. Riley was already a hundred yards along the trail to the summit, looking back over his shoulder. I had hiking boots and a full water bottle. Riley had yet to lead me astray.

The trail cut steeper and narrower than in California, lined with trees that sprouted dense, leafy foliage that was rusting and falling to the ground. A breeze stirred the branches, making a soft rustle as the still-clinging leaves did their best to hold on despite the inevitable. I swatted at a black fly buzzing by my face. A small trickle of sweat ran down between my shoulder blades. The air smelled damp, like rotting leaves, and mud, and decaying fallen logs. So different from California's scent of sage, bay, and eucalyptus that cleaning products mimicked for freshness. Riley trotted ahead, dodging between trees, yet keeping a vigilant eye on me. The trail opened up to a field of large boulders that looked as if someone had dropped a handful of rocks on the top of the mountain, like chocolate sprinkles on a sundae. White trail blazes sliced up the middle in a beeline for the summit. Bounding ahead, Riley skillfully picked his way through the boulder field, at times placing each of his paws on separate rocks. I scrambled after him in a crab walk.

On the summit, Riley sat king-of-the-mountain style on a flat rock, nose tipped slightly into the air like a hood ornament surveying the land below. From here, you could see the natural valley and why it made sense to dam the river. Tracing the fingers of the lake, I found the grey farmhouse roof looking like a postage stamp. Beverly's house sat only a few klicks over and beyond, scattered like toys, were roofs of neighbors I had yet to meet. There wasn't even a hint of a shadow of the town under the lake.

The afternoon sun reflected off the water, making it appear as an aquamarine jewel in the middle of an autumn landscape. I hadn't been working on any new jewelry designs in Maine, which was unlike me, or at least the me I used to know. I longed to reground myself in my beads and glass and silver. The blue of the water was unearthly, and the colorful pockets of changing trees between solid green pine forest harmonized together. I knew at once the piece I would make to capture it.

Then it came to me with absolute clarity. Lauren knew about Claire's pregnancy. She knew who my father was. And she knew why Claire had given me up. The ground tilted for a moment. My vision narrowed and I bent over, bracing myself on my knees. I breathed in and held it, squeezing my hands into fists. I exhaled slowly, like a tire losing its air.

★ ★ ★

Riley and I were snuggled on the couch reading after dinner when the doorbell rang. The start of the piece I envisioned on the top of Mount Bascom lay in progress on the dining-room table. I looked through the peephole expecting Beverly or Lucas, but instead Lauren stood on the front porch. I felt my heart in my chest.

"I'm sorry to just drop by like this," she said. Riley ran to his toy basket and brought her his favorite stuffed hedgehog. Lauren nervously fingered the collar of her coat.

"It's okay," I said.

"Claire," she started, then stopped.

"Do you want to sit down?" I asked.

She shook her head. "Claire entrusted this to me about thirty years ago." Lauren held a blue composition book in her hand with the words Godfrey College embossed on the front. "With the instructions that if anything ever happened to her, I was to give it to you." She shook her head. "We were so young. I never thought it would come to this."

She extended the book to me. I reached out to take it.

"No one," she said, staring into my eyes, not yet releasing her grip. "No one," she repeated, "besides me, and Claire, has ever read it. Do you understand?"

The small hairs on the back of my neck stood up. I nodded.

Lauren took a deep breath. "I will support whatever decision you make." And with that she transferred the blue composition book from her hands to mine.

CHAPTER THIRTEEN

Claire

Journal Entry, Jan Plan 1993

To break up the monotony of winter and to prevent any Shiningesque episodes from occurring in its dorms, Godfrey offered what they termed "Jan Plan" between the holidays and the official start of second semester. During the month of January, everyone either took a concentrated class, held an out-of-town internship, or studied language in a foreign country. Yet even with the dorms and dining halls half emptied, and campus more sparsely populated, the intensive nature of the month froze suspended like an ice cap over campus, putting everyone on edge.

This Jan Plan, Sloan interned at a Manhattan law firm, Will represented the UK in the Model UN, Trey studied the winter nesting habits of the Golden Eagle, Lauren traveled to Italy, and I signed up for a poetry class, mistakenly thinking that if I understood poetry, I would like it better. I admit to being relieved that Sloan was off campus and I would not have to face her for another month. Will, Trey, and I fell into a rhythm, and I found myself filing the last week with Trey away in the same place I shoved memories of my parents, as if it were all happening to a character in a novel that I could pick up or put down as I desired—until cracks appeared in the ice.

I recognized Trey's rap on my door on a random Tuesday night as I struggled through my used copy of the *Norton Anthology of Poetry*. My heart clenched for a beat. We had an agreement he would not visit my room alone. I cracked the door. Trey pushed past me, followed by Will and a wave of alcohol. They were dressed like arctic explorers in thick down jackets, wool scarves, gloves, and hats pulled low over their ears, not uncommon attire for January in Maine, but they looked more ready for snow camping on Mount Katahdin than the usual late-night caffeine-driven stroll across campus to the Coffee House.

"Hurry up," Trey said. "Tee time is at 11:00 p.m."

"What?"

"Snow golf. Dress warmly." His eyes were too bright and glassy.

Rosy-cheeked, Will held a five-iron over his shoulder like a fishing pole and a can of tennis balls.

I narrowed my eyes. "You're drunk."

"It's tradition." Trey passed me a flask of something that smelled like lighter fluid.

"No thanks."

"It'll warm you up." He shook it at me.

I ignored Trey, pulled on my layers and pushed them out the door ahead of me. Outside on fraternity row, thousands of frozen snow crystals reflected the bright moon off their surfaces and the night was absolutely still, as if trying to catch its breath in the thin air. My nostrils froze and the cold penetrated my thick jacket, pressed through my flannel and turtleneck, past my long underwear, and down to my skin. Even without windchill, it was well below freezing.

Trey set his tennis ball on the snow in the frosty halo of the porch light below the dorm steps, took the club in his gloved hands, and squared his shoulders. "First hole is the flagpole in front of the library. Par Three."

He took a swing, made awkward by his many layers, and the tennis ball flew toward its intended target, the dayglow yellow bright against the moonlit snow. "Booyah!"

He handed me the club. "Your turn."

I stepped up to the ball, trying to remember my father's lessons before I had declared golf too boring of a sport. My breath was visible against the cold, and my arms felt stiff.

"Let me help you." Trey wrapped his body around me from behind and gripped the club over my hands.

I tensed.

"Hands off my woman." Will shoved Trey's shoulder a little too hard in what I wanted to be alcoholic misjudgment.

Trey stepped away from me and, hands on hips, squared himself to Will.

"Your woman? You're too pansy-assed to satisfy a woman like Claire."

Will jabbed him in the chest and smirked as if delivering the perfect retort.

"That's not what she said." He laughed.

The moon reflected off the darkened windows of the nearly empty dorm standing guard and casting an impenetrable façade. Trey slapped Will's finger away.

"Enough." I separated them, a hand centered on each of their chests. "I've got this."

I stepped up to the makeshift tee, swung the club, and the ball soared straight toward the flagpole. Both of their heads followed its trajectory.

"We have a ringer," Will said.

"I'll say," Trey agreed.

At the third hole, the main brick dining hall to the warming hut by the skating pond, Trey slouched against the wrought-iron railing, a line of stunning yet lethal icicles behind him waiting to pierce an unsuspecting passerby.

When I stepped up for my turn, he said, "The way you grip that shaft is very sexy." He took another swig from the flask.

"Dude," Will said, packing snow between his gloves, winding up like a professional pitcher and hurling it at him. "I know you're not getting any this month, but *that's my girlfriend*." He emphasized the last three words.

Trey threw up his arms to block his face, and the snowball exploded against his elbow. "That's what you think," Trey said.

I stared at the row of icicles, imagined gripping the deadly spike nearly as thick as a baseball bat and breaking it off.

"Boys," I said quietly. "If you keep this up, you're going to be golfing alone." I held the club out. "Will, you're up. Hit the goddamn ball."

"Gimme that flask." Will snatched the container from Trey and tipped it to his lips.

By the time we reached the fifth hole, the Health Center to the front door of the chapel, the boys were starting to weave, the deep snow hindering their staggering, posthole steps but also helping hold them upright.

As Will readied himself to hit the ball, Trey said, "She's in love with me."

Will squinted at Trey, as if trying to bring him into focus.

"She's in love with me," Trey repeated.

The sharpness of the cold burned my cheeks, and heat flamed across my face. "Quiet," I said through clenched teeth.

Trey raised his voice so that it echoed off the dirty snow plowed up against the side of the Health Center. "I said, she's," he pointed at me with his club, "in love with me."

He fell over into the snow bank.

"What the hell?" Will bent over, bracing his hands on his knees as if about to throw up.

Trey struggled to get his feet underneath him.

"He's drunk," I said. "You're both drunk."

Will ran at Trey and tackled him back into the snow. "Why're you being such an asshole?" he yelled.

Trey thrashed against Will, both of them thick in their layers of clothing. Trey started swinging and kicking at Will, and Will punched back. They rolled around in the snow like two angry sumo wrestlers locked in a title fight, both trying to land a solid hit.

"Stop it!" I yelled. "Just stop it." I pelted them with the tennis balls.

"This is ridiculous. I should leave you both here to freeze to death." I grabbed Will by the back of his coat and tried without success to pull him up.

"Trey, you're going home, and Will, you're coming with me. Get up. Now!"

I kicked at them. Once they were standing, I looped my arms through theirs, like Dorothy with the Scarecrow and the Tin Man, but instead of skipping down the yellow brick road, we lurched along the plowed pathway to the dorms, a thousand ice crystals reflecting the moon lighting our way.

I deposited Trey at their shared dorm room where he staggered a few steps and collapsed face first onto his bed. Still in his thick jacket and boots, he tugged at the wool scarf around his neck, grunted, and gave up. I forced him to sit up and drink a glass of water, unraveling his scarf and pulling off his jacket and boots, then positioned the metal trash can along the side of the bed. Trey rolled onto his back and started snoring.

Will sat slumped on his own bed, face cradled in his hands, half-asleep, if not fully. I debated leaving him there but didn't want to risk it. I tugged Will to his feet, and he leaned on me, steadying himself for the few hundred yards to my dorm. Once in my room, Will shed his clothes, then slid along the hallway wall to the bathroom in his t-shirt and boxers. He took so long I wondered if he had passed out, but he eventually returned with his hair and face damp with water.

"Did you throw up?"

He nodded.

"Good."

He crawled into my twin bed, spooning around me, and squeezed. He was too warm and smelled like sweat and booze.

"Is there something we need to talk about?" he asked into the back of my neck.

"Go to sleep."

His breath deepened and his hold relaxed around my body. I lay awake for hours staring at the pale strip of hallway light beneath my doorway, wanting to flatten myself, slip under the door undetected, and escape.

★ ★ ★

The next morning, I left Will snoring softly in my bed with the sheets twisted around him. I could only hope that both boys had had so much alcohol they wouldn't remember what they'd said. Sitting on the wooden bench in front of the warming hut by the edge of the frozen pond, I tightened the laces of the battered white figure skates I'd borrowed from the Outing Club. As a Californian, I took being outside year-round for granted and had not realized how much the outdoors was part of me until the first serious snowfall in November.

When practice moved inside (Godfrey's indoor track and swimming pool the first I had ever seen), I learned the only way to survive cabin fever was to find new outdoor activities. Mainers were well-versed in winter sports, even ice fishing, which just seemed like an excuse for men to drink themselves blind in a ramshackle shelter on the ice where women had no interest in searching for them. In addition to my weekend cross-country skiing, I took up recreational ice skating. My skills were a lifetime behind the New Englanders, who grew up skating on ponds until they had blue lips and the beginnings of frostbite and could glide as effortlessly as they ran, changing direction without thinking.

I skated forward only, somewhat unsteadily around the cleared surface, my dull skate edges bumping over the bits of cattails and pond grass caught frozen in the ice surface, and breathed the fresh air. I was alone on the pond. After spending three laps focused on gliding across the ice while not flailing my arms, I looked to the shore and saw Trey sitting on the bench lacing up his hockey skates. A small bit of smoke curled from the warming-hut chimney behind him. He lifted his hand in a half wave, which I ignored.

Trey stepped onto the ice with the ease of a kid who played pond hockey until his mother called him into supper and angled to me. I kept skating in my loop away from him.

"Claire," he said, cutting me off with a perfect stop.

Unable to halt, I ran into him and had to grab his arms to balance myself, but I dropped my hold as soon as I stabilized.

"I'm sorry," he said.

"What the hell were you thinking?" I pushed off away from him.

"Claire," he called after me.

Trey quickly caught up and glided alongside until he forced me to look at him by skating backward in front of me, like an Olympic pair skater. "I want to be with you, Claire."

"That's not going to happen."

"Why not?"

"It's just not," I said.

Trey placed his lips against my ear. "I know you feel it too."

I suppressed a shiver, staring at him. "No," I said. "I don't."

"What did Will say to you?"

"Nothing."

He ran his fingers through his hair and tugged at his bangs, pressing his palm against his forehead.

"Make it right with him," I said.

He looked at me. "Are you going back to him?"

"You know what I learned this January? Two roads diverged in a wood and I, I took the one less travelled by."

I left Trey standing in the center of the ice, as I skated to the warming hut.

CHAPTER FOURTEEN

Claire

JOURNAL ENTRY, FEBRUARY 1993

"What the heck happened over Jan Plan?" Lauren asked at breakfast. She had just returned to campus and still had an Italian glow about her.

"What do you mean?" I sipped my orange juice.

"You're avoiding looking at the Royals."

"Am I?" I frowned.

"Don't play innocent with me." She reached across the table and flicked my shoulder.

I glanced to where Trey and Sloan sat looking tousled and satisfied, as if they'd just rolled out of bed after epic sex. Will was absent.

"I'm just taking a break." I pushed my eggs around my plate, then stopped and focused on her.

"Plus I haven't seen you in over a month and I want to hear about Florence and this Giovanni guy."

Lauren clasped her hand to her breast and sighed. "What is it about Italian men?" She kissed her pinched fingers. "Wait, nice distraction."

Lauren scooted her chair forward and lowered her voice. "Did Will break up with you?"

I took a deep breath. "Truth be told, I broke up with him."

"Let me get this straight." She leaned back and examined me over the rim of her coffee mug. "You broke up with the guy everyone wants."

"You don't want him."

"You're right." Lauren set down her cup. "I've always been partial to Trey."

My eggs caught halfway down my throat. "So Giovanni?" I raised my eyebrows.

"Not Giovanni until you've spilled it first."

"It just got too complicated," I said. "I told him I needed some space to sort out how I was feeling."

"And he accepted that?"

I took a bite of my scrambled eggs and shrugged. "I played the dead-parents card."

★ ★ ★

Indoor-track season started in earnest in February, and Lauren and I spent hours sprinting around the track, bundling up for long, slow mileage outside, lifting light weights to build strength, and running suspended in the deep end of the pool to give our legs a break from the frozen ground.

"While you were busy cross-country skiing yourself into perfect form, I was stuffing myself with pasta and chianti," she said, huffing beside me.

Between track and my full course load, I saw very little of Will, Trey, and Sloan, but that didn't stop the rumors from circulating. Each day Lauren came to practice she had a new one. "I overheard in French today that Will dumped you because your father works for the CIA and he threatened to have him killed." She propped her long leg up on the railing outside the field house and stretched to her toes.

"Don't people have anything better to talk about?"

"Apparently not." We started off down the plowed sidewalk at an easy pace, today being a long slow distance day to build our base. "Yesterday's is still my favorite."

"That I'm a prostitute working for the Russian Mafia?"

"You do know a lot about the Soviet Union."

"It's my minor."

"Just sayin'." She held out her arms, palms up in the picture of innocence, keeping an easy stride next to me.

"I'm glad one of us is enjoying this."

We ran in silence past the snow-covered soccer fields, down the hill from which Godfrey overshadowed the mill town of Babcock Falls, and out along the wooded roads surrounding the college, heading in the direction of Lone Loon Pond. When we reached the campsite parking lot a few miles later, we stopped and stretched against the picnic tables. Just being there made me feel the same sense of calmness I experienced skiing around the pond in solitude over the holidays, but Lauren seemed a bit out of sorts.

"You've been awfully quiet," I said.

Lauren stared out at the frozen lake with her hands on her hips, then turned to face me with a serious expression. "You know you can tell me anything, right?"

I studied the familiar spattering of freckles across her flushed pink cheeks. Her eyebrows were pulled together in concern. From our first meeting, Lauren had accepted me as I was, and I trusted her completely. I opened my mouth, but my voice caught in my throat. I pictured my moose.

"I've been sleeping with Trey."

"What?" She plopped onto the picnic-table bench.

"Since the first week of school."

"Wow." Lauren scratched under her knit hat and then turned to look at me. "How'd that even happen?"

I told her about the tent and the rain.

"Does Will know?"

I pulled my heel up to my butt and stretched my quad. "Not that he's allowing himself to admit."

"You need to give me a minute to digest this." Lauren studied me. "You can really keep a secret."

"Will's a good guy. I don't want to hurt him."

"That's why you broke up with him."

I nodded. "Trey wants to be together."

"Sloan?"

I shrugged.

"Is the sex amazing? Tell me it's amazing." She waved her hand. "Never mind, the color your face just turned answered that."

"It's the only time I've felt free since my parents' death."

Lauren stood and jumped a few times to ready herself for the return run. "I guess this pond isn't the only one hiding something under its frozen surface."

★ ★ ★

I ran into Will coming out of the field house toward the end of the month. He held the door for me. "Hi," he said.

I had only seen him at a distance. Even though it was a small campus and our dorms were near each other, it was surprisingly easy to avoid someone. Probably easier when that person was also avoiding you. "Hi."

"How've you been?" His dark hair fell into his eyes, giving him a sheep-dog look. He pushed it out of the way.

I folded my arms. "Good. And you?"

"Good."

We stared at each other in silence. "Ok, well, I'm heading up to dinner." I exited past him.

"Wait," he grabbed my arm. I turned to face him. "We're still friends, right?"

"I hope so," I said.

"Can we hang out tonight?"

"Yes." I relaxed. "I'd like that."

And that was how I found myself sneaking a tray from the dining hall and standing at the top of Chapel Hill with Will. He placed his tray on the snow and sat on top of it, bracing himself from sliding down the hill with his feet. I copied him.

"How do I stop?" I asked.

"You don't," he said. "Just try to avoid hitting the light pole down there at the bottom and you'll be fine."

We slid down the hill, the slick industrial plastic of the trays making a surprisingly efficient sled. I gripped the lip of the tray with my mittened hands, and not only did I manage to not fall off, but I was able to steer by leaning my weight in the direction I wanted to go. When the hill flattened, I braked with the heels of my boots. Grinning, I turned to face Will. "Let's go again."

We trudged to the top of the hill and rode down at least ten times before coming to a final rest at the bottom.

"Thank you," I said. "I needed that."

Will packed snow between his gloved hands. "I've missed you, Claire."

"I've missed you too."

"Trey said . . ." He let his voice drift off.

"Trey said, what?" My neck prickled.

He threw his packed snowball at the lamp post but missed. "To stay away from you. To give you space." Will started forming another snowball.

"Did he say anything else?"

"Just to pick a few of the other hundred women who want to have sex with me and move on." He grinned. This time his snowball hit the lamppost and Will raised his arms signaling a touchdown.

"Charming," I said.

"I get you've had a rough time, but I'd like to go back to being friends if you're up for it."

"I'd like that," I said. "I'd like that very much."

★ ★ ★

Sloan cornered me in the stairwell of the English Building. "How was your Jan Plan?" I asked, smile plastered on face.

"You should get back together with Will," she said.

"Why's that?" I folded my arms across my chest.

"So we can all focus on other things."

"I'm surprised you want me around."

"I'm trying to be nice here, Claire. Work with me."

I took a deep breath and exhaled.

"I don't know what happened over Jan Plan." She pressed me into the corner. "But Will's been moping around and Trey just seems bitter. You broke it. You need to fix it."

Sloan stepped back and turned to walk down the stairs. "They're singing tonight in the CoHo. Come."

"Careful what you ask for," I called to her retreating back.

★ ★ ★

I dragged Lauren with me to the CoHo, having explained the situation to her at practice. We arrived right as they darkened the lights and Looking for Treble took the stage. We ordered coffee and glanced around for a place to sit. As usual, it was packed with women perched on the edges of their seats like vultures, looking as if they wanted to devour the guys on stage. Sloan sat in her usual booth, which I'd learned was called the Queen's Throne, and beckoned me over when I inadvertently caught her eye. I grasped Lauren by the wrist and pulled her with me. We slid into the booth. Sloan and Lauren nodded at each other.

My heart raced as if I were on the final lap of the 1500

meter. Watching Will and Trey from the safety of the dark booth, much as I had from across the glow of the campfire, I wondered if I would have acted differently that night if I had known Trey was off limits. I couldn't take my eyes from him, overwhelmed by a surge of memories about the feel of his body against mine, the taste of his skin, and the combination of desire and abandon and desperation that overtook his features when we lost ourselves in each other. Studying his face as he sang, I replayed all of our encounters and fantasized new ones.

After their performance, Trey and Will came over to the booth. "Hi Lauren," Trey said. "Claire," he nodded at me. They sat down across from us.

"What'd you think?" Will asked.

"You guys sound even better than you did at Exeter," Lauren said.

"I need some caffeine," Trey said. "Anyone else?" Will and Sloan nodded. "Join me, Claire." It wasn't a question.

"Sure," I said. Lauren dug her nails into my leg under the table. "I need a cookie."

Trey waited for me to slide out of the booth and then followed me to the counter. His fury daggered my back. "Sloan asked me to come," I said. "What did you want me to say?"

"You didn't have to say yes."

"No," I said. "I didn't."

He smiled at me and widened his eyes, casting them back to the table. I glanced back and saw all three of them watching. I matched his facial expression. At the counter we stood shoulder to shoulder, our faces blocked from view.

"Why don't you just stay away from Will?"

"You think that will solve things?"

"It would be a start."

"Between us, or between me and Will?" I said.

"You made it clear there was no us."

I glanced around to see who was listening and lowered my voice. "Tell me one thing," I said. "Why did you start this?"

"I didn't just want to sit across the table staring at you."

"I'm talking about the tent."

The barista placed the order on the counter and Trey wrapped his hands around the cups. He jerked his head. "Let's get back to the table."

"I'm not going to stop being friends with Will just because you can't handle it."

Trey stared at me.

"Sloan wants us back together."

"Us?"

I rolled my eyes. "Me and Will."

He hesitated and then looked into his coffee. "I broke up with Sloan."

"It doesn't look that way." I gestured back to the table.

"She just doesn't want to accept it."

"Does she know about us?"

"I'm not stupid," he said. "But neither is she. Let's go."

When we returned to the table, Lauren and Will were mocking a teacher they'd had at Exeter. Even Sloan was laughing.

"No cookie?" Will said.

"Oh," I said. "I decided I didn't need one."

"What if I needed one?"

"Too bad." I hoped my laugh only sounded forced to me.

CHAPTER FIFTEEN

Claire

JOURNAL ENTRY, ST. PATRICK'S DAY 1993

The fact that Saint Patrick's Day fell on a Saturday night didn't help. The dining hall served corned beef and cabbage, and there was no shortage of green beer, Boston Celtics' wear, and the Pogues playing on repeat at the various preparties, but the main event was an all-campus shindig in the Student Center that began at 10:00 p.m. Lauren and I started by doing shots of green-tinted grain alcohol with the track team in one of the frat houses. I wore a green shirt and a *Kiss Me I'm Irish* button, and Lauren had on a leprechaun hat. We'd won our track meet that day, a matchup we hadn't been expected to come out ahead in, and the team was celebrating harder than usual. Nothing is worse than a bunch of already-too-skinny runners rehydrating with Everclear.

We made it to the Student Center by 11:00 p.m., the party already raging in full force. The hot, sour smell of alcohol-soaked bodies assaulted us as we pushed through the heavy door. They checked our IDs, but everyone knew if you put your wristband on loosely you could slip it off for someone underage and get yourself another. The Student Center had multiple cascading tiers, so that standing on the dance floor was like being on center stage at a grand theater, the patrons in their box seats gazing down at the performers through opera glasses. Like the theater, the audience could see across one side of the half-moon to the other, noting who watched from which tier. Unlike the theater, people dropped beers over the balconies, adding to the already sticky dance floor. Dark corners hid those who wanted to avoid being seen.

Twinkle lights dimly lit the room, and the DJ spun the latest dance hits—Salt N' Pepa and Run DMC back-to-back with Marky Mark and Madonna. Green streamers and shamrocks were pasted to the walls, and emerald Mardi Gras beads draped over the balconies. A line for green beer snaked through one swinging door into the kitchen and out the other and, as long as you had a wristband, you could take two beers at a time.

As with every other part of its alcohol policy, Godfrey wanted the pretense of regulation, but didn't want the regulations to actually get in the way of anyone drinking. Everyone traveled on foot, there was nowhere to drive, and the more attractive the school could make its sponsored party, the less likely to have incidents elsewhere. Sort of like those parents in high school who let kids drink at their house because they knew they were going to drink somewhere, so they might as well make it as safe as possible. Plus Godfrey prided itself on being one of *U.S. News and World Report's* Top 25 Liberal Arts Colleges in the country, and student happiness weighed significantly in keeping its place (and bragging rights) ahead of Colby and Bowdoin. Needless to say, the Health Center staff was well-versed in treating alcohol poisoning.

Lauren and I pushed our way through students clogging the stairway onto the dance floor. People sang at the top of their lungs to Meatloaf's "Paradise by the Dashboard Light" and thrashed about like they were having seizures. We joined in and lost ourselves to the music. Heat radiated off the sweaty bodies despite the gaping windows behind the DJ on the stage. Packed together, barely enough room to dance in place, the floor sticky, I spun with my arms above my head enjoying the lightness supplied by the leprechaun punch. I tipped my head back, scanning the balconies, and caught Trey watching me over the rim of his green plastic cup from the third floor. He was alone. Our eyes met and he lifted his chin in a slight nod. Will appeared by his side, and Trey said something into his ear. His gaze followed Trey's pointed finger, then he toasted me. When I spun around again, they were gone.

The grain alcohol had gone down easily, too easily. I felt euphoric. I'd run a personal best in the two-mile, beating the women from Smith who had managed to stay one step ahead of me all cross-country season, and contributing to the extra points we hadn't expected to win. The whole team had done well, hence the exuberant preparty. Several teammates had joined us on the dance floor, and everyone pogoed to House of Pain. A smooth buzz, energized, carefree, and completely present, enjoying my teammates and basking in the win—a perfect moment.

I felt a hand on the small of my back, and then Will bounced in front of me smiling a wide grin. Lauren's eyes bugged. Trey materialized at my side, nodding to the beat and holding his hand over his cup so as not to spill. They both wore green beads and Will had on shamrock suspenders. Trey tossed back his beer, and the track team absorbed them into our pack. Everyone danced and twirled and threw their bodies about as if this were all that mattered.

The crowd engulfed Will and pressed Trey against me. His body heat radiated through my shirt, and his familiar scent intoxicated me. A slow song came on. Sweat dripped down my back and I lifted my hair off my neck. I wanted nothing more than to wrap myself around Trey like cellophane, and his face mirrored my feelings. Will slow-danced with one of the women from my team a few feet away. Trey mimed getting another beer and I followed him off the dance floor. Once out of Will's sight, he entwined his fingers in mine and pulled me to the kitchen, but instead of getting in the beer line he ducked into the pantry and locked the door behind us.

Despite the industrial-metal racks of dry goods, most of the student body right outside the door, and the hundreds of reasons it was a bad idea, we attacked each other, yanking at clothing, pressing up against shelves, and every breath, every touch, every desire became so urgent it felt as if we needed to be fused together in order to live.

Afterward, we lay side by side on our backs, sticky and sweating on the cold tile floor.

"That was insane," Trey said, once we'd caught our breaths.

I laced my fingers through his and squeezed. "We need to get back out to the dance floor."

He didn't move. "I think I'm in love with you."

"Don't say that."

"Why not?"

"I just can't handle it right now."

We lay still for another few minutes and then began putting ourselves back together. We slipped out of the pantry and rejoined the track team on the dance floor, still buzzing from both the alcohol and our encounter. The smell of Trey and sex engulfed me, but no one seemed the wiser. That night I drank copious amounts of water before going to bed.

★ ★ ★

At first my mind couldn't make sense of the eerie cry of bagpipes haunting my dreams. I wrestled myself from sleep, sat up, and lifted the corner of the window blind by the bed. A heavy mist hung over the field that stretched from my dorm to the pond. It was barely daybreak. My head felt fuzzy, but remarkably good considering the leprechaun punch from the night before. I pulled boots on over the wool socks I slept in, wrapped myself in my heavy coat, and followed the siren call. Campus sat in hushed silence. Significant patches of dirty snow spotted the landscape, but bare ground and muddied dead grass now lay exposed ready for spring. With my hood pulled up and my hands stuffed in the pockets of my coat, I picked my way through the snow-pocked field to the pond. The bagpipes' cry permeated the fog and transported me to the Moors of Scotland during an earlier century. The heavy mist felt damp on my cheeks, swallowing the brick buildings behind me so that I walked blindly into a timeless druidic plane until the pond's familiar warming hut materialized out of the fog. I sat on the bench.

Across the pond I could make out a figure dressed in a kilt and tam-o'-shanter, most likely an eccentric professor still drunk on Irish whiskey, who woke to the mist and felt the pull. The bagpipes' melancholy song tugged at the loss I tried to keep trapped deep inside me, and I felt tears begin to drip down my cheeks. I didn't bother to wipe them away but sat and listened to the voice that spoke to me. I cried not only for my parents, but for the loss of the person I was before they died, and the confusion about who I was now. Slowly a few other figures dressed in odd layers emerged from the mist, drawn from their warm beds by the same call. We remained separate, held together only by the lonely and haunting melody piercing through the fog.

★ ★ ★

While I wept for all that I had lost, a girl walking back from her boyfriend's room found the cold, stiff body of Chip Gavin, captain of the football team, in the melting snow at the base of the library clock tower. Campus Security and the Babcock Falls Police Department determined the cause of death to be a broken neck from a fall from the roof. His blood-alcohol level was 0.15%. As the news spread, a hush fell over the dining hall during breakfast, everyone clumped together in whispered conversations to speculate.

"My God, did you hear?" I plunked myself down at the Royal's table with Will, Trey, and Sloan.

"Yeah, it's awful," Will said. He looked clammy and slightly nauseous. Trey powered through his cereal as if he hadn't eaten in days.

"What do you think he was doing on the roof?"

Will shrugged and Trey ignored me. They ate their breakfast in silence.

"You guys hung over?" I asked.

"It was a rough night." Trey didn't look up from his Raisin Bran.

I glanced at Sloan. "I didn't see you at the party."

"I wasn't feeling social." She looked pointedly at Trey.

"Anyone else hear the bagpipes this morning?" I asked.

"No, I was alone in my room," Sloan said, now glaring at Trey.

"We were alone in our room too," Trey said.

"Yeah, after we left the party we went straight home," Will said.

The three of them returned to eating their breakfasts in silence. I should have known then, but instead I made an excuse about Lauren and moved to a table where several track team members sat rehashing the party and speculating about the accident like the rest of the room.

Later, when Will pounded on my door, all I could think was that he knew about me and Trey in the pantry. He pushed past me, his face flushed and eyes slightly wild, and sat on my bed with his head cradled in his hands.

"What's wrong?"

"It wasn't meant to happen." He rocked his head.

"You're scaring me."

Will looked up and locked eyes with me. "Can I trust you?"

"Of course."

"Can I really trust you?"

I sat down on the bed next to him and placed my hand on his shoulder. "Will, just tell me what happened."

"You cannot tell a living soul, do you understand? Ever."

"I promise."

"Okay, well you know how Trey's father is?" He waited until I nodded. "He wouldn't let it alone that Trey needed to retaliate."

The pieces clicked together and my neck tingled. I didn't want to hear what came next.

"Trey found a list of the current members of Alpha Tau stuck in the historical records they keep in this locked room in the library. We couldn't believe our luck that they were dumb enough to write it down. We made a copy, and then we sent an anonymous note to the president of Alpha Tau telling him to meet us on the balcony of the library clock tower after the Saint Patrick's Day party. We were drunk, all three of us. You know, you saw me and Trey."

I nodded.

"Trey taunted him with the list and he tried to snatch it away. They struggled." Will closed his eyes. "Trey's hands were on his throat, and he kept punching Trey, and then it was like he just lifted up and went over the side. He didn't even scream. I was standing there, staring at his crumpled body when Trey grabbed me and shoved me back down the stairway. I wanted to report it, but Trey called his dad. All I know is after Chaz Price got involved, it was ruled an accident and our names haven't been mentioned."

"It was an accident."

Will shook his head. "You don't know Trey like I do. Sometimes the pressure gets to him. He is his father's son."

"Are you telling me it was intentional?"

He pulled at his hair.

"Will, what are you saying?" I felt sick. "Will?"

He stared at me. "If you could have seen the look in his eyes."

"Does Sloan know?"

Will shook his head again.

"You can't tell anyone, including Trey, and you have to act naturally."

CHAPTER SIXTEEN

Claire

Journal Entry, April Fools 1993

If I had known that my outdoor track meet would be snowed out on April first, that would have felt like enough of a joke for having chosen to come to New England from California, but when I missed my period, I knew who was the biggest fool. Trey and I had been careless Saint Patrick's Day, but I had shoved the thought from my mind. The Health Center confirmed the home-pregnancy test results and handed me some brochures on my choices.

No matter how much I wasn't ready to be a mother, I sure as hell wasn't terminating my only living relative. I wouldn't be showing by the end of May, and I would finish my senior year in California. No one in Maine would be the wiser. It was a simple plan, which would have worked if morning sickness had been easier to hide from a smart woman looking to confirm her suspicions.

The day before Spring Break, I sat next to Sloan, the Caldwells, and the Prices on the rigid metal bleachers trying to watch the boy's ECAC Championship lacrosse game against Bowdoin. The families had not been told yet about their breakup, and Sloan wanted to keep it that way. Trey and Sloan had exchanged heated words by the stairway in the field house before the game. I was stretching in the foyer after my run and, even though I couldn't initially hear what they said, their body language told me enough.

When Trey tried to walk away, Sloan followed. "If you really break up with me, so help me God, you'll regret it," Sloan said within earshot. Trey gave her a withering stare, then caught sight of me frozen at the railing. Sloan followed his look. "And you will too," she said.

After the game, the families took us to dinner at the nicest restaurant in town, a converted farmhouse where we sat in a cozy, candlelit front room that housed only a few other tables. Over the main course, Charles Price, wearing a plastic bib adorned with a picture of a lobster and brandishing a nut cracker, turned to me. "What are your plans after graduation, Claire?"

They were well into the fourth bottle of wine, and no one seemed to notice I still sipped at my first glass.

"I'm only a junior," I said. "I'll be returning to California to finish my senior year."

"You are?" Trey said.

"It's a one-year exchange program. You know that."

Sloan studied us.

"I bet Will is disappointed about that," Mrs. Price said, looking at Will. Apparently there were two relationships the Prices had not been updated about.

"And these two," Mr. Caldwell waved his glass at Trey and Sloan, "will be engaged soon."

"Daddy," Sloan said.

"I know, the wedding will need to wait until after you graduate from Harvard Law, but we'll get you a place together on Beacon Hill. These days there's no reason to wait until you're married to live together." Mr. Caldwell winked at his wife. "Not like it was in our generation."

Charles Price turned to Trey. "Have you and Will finalized

your itinerary for Europe? I always say it's important to sow some wild oats before you settle down."

"Chaz," Mrs. Price said.

There was a beat too long of silence, during which both Sloan and I willed Trey to keep his mouth shut. Trey swirled his red wine, staring into the glass as if expecting to see his fortune told. "Sloan and I broke up."

Sloan sat straighter in her chair and narrowed her eyes.

"I'm sure you had a disagreement, but you'll work it out," Mrs. Caldwell squeezed Sloan's hand. Sloan snatched it away.

"Maybe I'll move to California." Trey looked pointedly at me.

Sloan looked as if she'd been slapped, and Will's head jerked up.

"The land of fruits and nuts," Charles Price said.

"You're joking," Mr. Caldwell said. "You two are getting married. Kiss and make up. End of discussion."

"Daddy," Sloan said.

"I'm not sure we can do that, sir," Trey said.

Sloan's father turned on her. "What did you do?"

"I didn't do anything!"

"Well you must have done something."

Sloan's face turned an unnatural shade of red. "Ask him what *he* did."

Sloan leveled a finger at Trey. Will pushed back his chair to better see Trey beside him. Trey glanced across at me. I felt as if I balanced on a wobbling tight rope.

"Don't look at her." Sloan pushed her chair away from the table and stood up.

"Honey, I'm sure you're just overreacting," Charles Price said to Sloan.

"Overreacting?" Sloan stood, hands on her hips.

"Claire's pregnant." The table looked at me. "And your son is the father."

I stared at my plate, wishing I could evaporate.

"What the hell are you talking about?" Trey pushed back from the table.

"Oh you didn't know? You thought that glow," she swirled her finger in the air in front of her face, "was just love for you?"

"What the fuck, dude?" Will said.

"Sloan," her mother tugged on her sleeve. "Sit down."

Sloan shook her off.

"Is it true?" Mrs. Price asked, studying me.

I closed my eyes and took deep, centering breaths just like the grief counselor taught me. I pictured my winter moose with his long eyelashes, liquid brown eyes of wisdom, and the majestic strength in his antlers while he quietly chewed the reeds.

"Claire?" Trey said.

"She's not even denying it," Sloan said.

"How much do you want to make this go away?" Charles Price asked.

I snapped my eyes open and stared at him. "I don't want anything from you. Ever." I folded my napkin and pushed back my chair.

"I'm sorry," I mouthed to Will. I picked up my coat and walked to the restaurant door.

"Where do you think you're going, young lady?" Mrs. Caldwell called after me.

"Let her go," I heard Mrs. Price say.

A wet chill hung in the air, and the asphalt was slick with black ice. I could see my breath. I buttoned my coat, pulled on my hat and gloves, and started the walk back to campus. The sky was ink-black with a smattering of bright stars. The restaurant light didn't reach beyond the parking lot, and a few steps down the driveway I receded into the darkness like a shadow. The front door to the farmhouse opened and threw a shaft of light, backlighting Trey. He caught me before I made it to the road. "Is it true?" he asked. "Is it mine?"

I stopped. "It's not Will's."

"Were you even going to tell me?"

"Truthfully, no."

"What the hell, Claire!"

"My body, my choice." I tried to step past him.

He grabbed my arm. "My parents won't want you to have an abortion."

"Tell them it's too late."

He ran his hand through his hair. "You don't know my parents, Claire. They will stop at nothing."

"That's what terrifies me. In my family, there was love and respect and my parents wanted nothing more than for me to follow my dreams. I miss them every day. I will not willingly bring a child into the ruthlessness of your family. I don't care how much money or influence they have." I shoved my hands in my pockets.

"I'm not like them, Claire." Trey held his arms out from his body, pleading. He wore a navy trench coat with the collar turned up. His cheeks were flushed and his hair ruffled. He looked so handsome. He blew into his bare hands and rubbed them together.

"How can you be so sure?"

"I'm my own person." Trey reached for my arm.

"The football captain might beg to differ."

His mouth dropped open and panic flashed across his face. "Did Will tell you?"

"That's what you're worried about? Who told me?"

"It was an accident, Claire." Trey reached for me again. "You have to believe me."

I shook him off.

"What are you going to do?"

"Whatever I have to." I pushed past him and didn't look back.

CHAPTER SEVENTEEN

Lindsay

It was the boldness of the act that struck me first, then the gumption she needed to get away with it. I reread the opening entry from May 1993 in Claire's blue composition book, trying to put myself in her shoes. How threatened, or desperate, or hopeless I would need to feel to come up with faking my own death as a practical solution to anything, but I didn't read about any of those feelings. Only simple shrewd resourcefulness. I sat back on the couch and took my first sip of wine since opening the notebook.

Riley snored from his dog bed in front of the fire's dying embers, having long ago given up on us climbing the stairs to bed. I marched to the office door and thrust it open, then fired up the computer. The password-protected login gave me brief pause before I typed "Riley" and was granted access. I watched the blinking curser on the search bar, fingers hovering above the keys. Up until this point I had not been ready to look behind the curtain, but now there was no going back.

I typed *Claire Sullivan* into the search engine, but didn't get the correct results until I tried *Lone Loon Pond Drowning 1993* and discovered her true last name. This started me down the yellow brick road that included stops at *declaring someone dead without a body, putting a baby up for adoption without father's consent*, and *how to conceal your identity.*

★ ★ ★

Standing at the top of the campground boat ramp the next morning, I shielded my eyes from the rising sun. The farmhouse was invisible, hidden in one of the curved fingers of the lake. The newspaper article had described the search-and-rescue team discovering the canoe tangled in the reeds along the eastern shore. The paddle floating a few hundred yards away. It also mentioned the Pan Am crash that made Claire an orphan. Her academic and athletic record at Godfrey. The rumored pregnancy. And a calculated quote from Lauren about how Claire hadn't been acting like herself the last few months.

Authorities had gone door-to-door to the camps surrounding the lake asking for information, and searched the shore for signs of Claire's whereabouts. After a few fruitless days the search was suspended. Claire was officially declared a missing person, presumed dead. I imagined a younger Claire and Lauren stretching against the picnic tables, and Will and Trey there after the kidnapping. I read the placard about how in 1950 the town that once sat in the valley was relocated and the river damned to bring much needed power to Central Maine.

As Claire ran from the shore in the cloak of darkness, did she imagine she would one day return to Lone Loon Pond? Or that I would?

★ ★ ★

Godfrey's Outing Club was headquartered at the campus pond, home to native waterfowl and surrounded by sloped grassy banks manicured by Godfrey's Buildings and Grounds Department—a scene so picturesque it appeared in the forefront of Godfrey's marketing photos. The iconic library clocktower loomed in the distance. The Outing Club still checked out boating equipment, camping gear, cross-country skis, and ice skates. I tried to picture the pond frozen solid and transformed into an outdoor ice rink but, as a Californian, seasonally shifting landscapes were not easy to imagine. Especially blanketed in snow.

Across the way, the weatherproof track encircled the football field in front of the main entrance to the Price Field House. I walked a lap envisioning Lauren and Claire flying around its curves in their racing spikes. From there, I made my way up frat row where L.L.Bean-clad students hurried to class. I briefly regretted not knowing which dorms Claire and Trey had lived in, but seeing the symmetrical brick houses sufficed. In the large columned building at the end of the row, I followed two outdoorsy coeds into the gothic dining hall that looked straight out of Harry Potter. Minus the floating candlesticks. The elevated section where the Royals presumably once sat remained intact by the floor-to-ceiling windows. Who sat there now?

Standing back from the entrance to the library, I tilted my head up to stare at the top of the infamous clock tower with its moose weathervane—at least a five-story fall with nothing to break it. I imagined a contorted chalk outline at my feet on the blacktop.

Trey wouldn't have lured the football captain onto the widow's walk if he weren't intending to threaten him with more than the list of names. My anger was always so short-lived. Expired as soon as it was expressed. I'd never thrown a punch in my life. Nor needed to. Either I had been spared that Price gene, or Trey's violence was a product of nurture.

Weaving through the library stacks, I trailed my fingers along spines of dusty books that likely hadn't been pulled from their shelves in fifty years. I asked the librarian behind the reference desk for information on the fraternities at Godfrey. She raised her eyebrows. When I explained my grandfather had been an alumnus and I was putting together a scrapbook for his seventieth birthday, she led me through the stacks to a discrete room with an open door that had glass cases filled with pictures and memorabilia from the fraternity days lining the walls. Most of the photos depicted the sixties and earlier, hairstyles and dress codes reflecting bygone eras, but some were from the decades immediately before the abolishment.

I came across a caption, *Theodore Charles "Chaz" Price, Junior,* and my breath caught. There, staring confidently into the camera, stood a lanky boy with his arms draped over the shoulders of two others identified as Alexander Caldwell and Henry Westin. My grandfather, with Sloan and Will's fathers. I saw no familiarity in his features and searched for menace in his eyes. The boys looked so young and full of life, sure of themselves and their places in the world. As if they knew they would do big things. The relationships they forged at Godfrey indeed lasting a lifetime as promised. I took a step back.

The room once sealed shut to the student body was now open for viewers. That history more than thirty years behind the school. Framed newspaper articles of the controversial decision, pictures of the angered members burning furniture on the lawn, and photos of women protesting sexual discrimination even hung on the walls. The archives, which gave an overview of the history of each of the fraternities once at Godfrey, had only two lines in the section about Alpha Tau, which read, *in an early 1990s incident, a majority of Godfrey football players were discovered to be associated with Alpha Tau underground fraternity. The fraternity was yet again abolished.*

I walked the long way, through the arboretum along the running trails where Claire and Lauren's relationship grew, to the top of Haskin's Hill where my parents first met. I emerged from the trees to an unremarkable grassy meadow that stretched down the hill, the closest building the corner of a dorm barely visible at the bottom of the long slope. Standing with my hands on my hips, I turned in a slow circle like the moose weathervane topping the library clock tower in the distance.

If only it hadn't rained.

★ ★ ★

I caught Lauren locking up the bookstore. One look at my face and she looped her arm through mine. "Let's have a glass of something."

We walked to the cafe in silence, our steps echoing in the still evening air. Once seated with our drinks, I fiddled with the candle in a habit that annoyed my mother, pressing my fingertip into the hot wax and leaving behind my print. I stared at my fingerprint a moment, a fingerprint that might not have existed, then looked up at Lauren.

"Tell me everything you know."

Lauren glanced around the cafe—she had seated us at a quiet table in the corner. Taking a deep breath, she told me the story she had been holding in for most of her adult life. She had waited twenty-four hours to call Campus Security to tell them Claire hadn't returned and she was worried.

"I didn't have to fake anything, I was worried, just not about what they thought."

Will and Trey hadn't been on speaking terms, but Claire's alleged death brought them back together. "Maybe not to where they were before, but enough," Lauren said. "That was one of Claire's goals. She knew the aftermath of a deadly accident. She calculated their reconciliation."

Graduation loomed only a few weeks away. Campus buzzed with seniors finalizing post-college plans. "When I saw Trey," Lauren said, "he was a hollow shell going through the motions. I didn't hear from Claire until after you were adopted."

Fear of the Prices finding her kept Claire from seeking refuge at her childhood home, which was already rented out while she finished college. Instead, Claire lived in the Napa Valley vacation property of her parent's attorney—a close family friend who had managed her affairs since their deaths—during her pregnancy. After quietly notifying the Maine State Police that Claire was alive, her attorney arranged for a closed adoption and Claire legally changed her last name.

"It's not a crime to go missing as an adult," Lauren said. "She just needed the Prices to believe her dead long enough to finalize the adoption."

"But wouldn't she have needed Trey's consent?"

"Not under certain circumstances. And her lawyer took care of that." Lauren took a sip of wine. "Afterward, Claire kept a low profile, working in wineries and restaurants where no one cared if she had finished college. When the Culinary Institute opened a school in Saint Helena, she discovered her passion. For the last ten years Claire ran the restaurant at the Belgrade Inn out on Great Pond. God, she loved it there, and they loved her." She shook her head. "Such an incredible loss."

"But why come back here? Wasn't she afraid of being found?"

"Honestly, I think this was the place she finally felt peace after her parents' death, so it was the place she sought after her husband died. Losing your parents young is awful enough, but losing your young husband too. She was devastated." Lauren shrugged.

"Plus, I was here and, by that point, you were an adult. Claire avoided Godfrey, and she lived and worked outside of Babcock Falls under a different last name. Trey and Sloan live in New York. In the worst-case scenario of them running into each other in town, Claire would have said she'd had a miscarriage from the stress of almost drowning. It was a closed adoption. Your birth records are sealed. It would have been very difficult to find you, even if they knew where to look."

"Yes, even I can't get my original birth certificate." I traced the stem of my wine glass.

"She went to such lengths to hide my birth."

"She believed it was worth it."

"Was it?"

"Homecoming is next weekend," Lauren said. "And Trey and Sloan are on the attending list."

I stared at the ceiling and steepled my fingers under my chin.

★ ★ ★

Finding information about a person not pretending to be dead proved much easier. Trey's social-media accounts and articles about him in the *Business Times* and local papers appeared with a few clicks. I stared at his photos for hours, squinting to see our similarities. The angle of his chin. The slope of a nose. His coloring. Trey was attractive for his age. Silver hair creeping from his temples, broad shoulders, and a trim build. I had never analyzed my own father's looks—he just looked like he looked. Tall, slender from behind, beer belly from the side, a comb-over, and a slightly red complexion. A suburban dad who had let himself go. And the alcohol didn't help.

Trey and Sloan married after graduate school and now had two children in high school, both accomplished athletes and academically successful, if social media was to be believed. My half-siblings. My friends with remarried parents often had significantly younger or older half-siblings who felt as distant as step-brothers and sisters. Half my genes had come from Trey and half theirs had too. Trey thought they were his only children. I could see Trey a little around their eyes and in their smiles, but otherwise they were pure Sloan. We would not be recognized as related.

Sloan had graduated from law school and worked for a top firm in New York, with Trey a partner at a hedge fund. They vacationed in the Hamptons and supported the local environmental organizations and the kids' schools. I came across an obituary for Chaz Price, who had recently died of a heart attack. I googled *heart attack, hereditary factors*. Eleanor Price had a lifetime of volunteer work in the community with the humanitarian awards to back it. She appeared in good health.

Their Concord home featured in architectural digests and interior-design magazines, and satellite pictures confirmed the property backed up to the conservation lands surrounding Walden Pond. I zoomed in, wondering what it would have been like going there for holidays since they would have been my only living grandparents, but all I could imagine were all the Williams' family traditions that were as ingrained in me as my genes.

I tried to wrap my head around the concept that I was looking at photos of my biological family. Not some random people on the internet. When driving in new areas I often imagined what it would be like to live there, but it was a game to pass time. These people who lived these full, complete lives on the opposite coast were fact, not fiction. They could have raised me. I had never gone seeking my birth parents, yet here on the internet existed my alternate life, displayed in photos, articles, and social media for all the world to see.

I googled *student clocktower death Godfrey 1993*. There was just a small paragraph in the local *Babcock Falls Gazette*, but as expected Trey's and Will's names were not mentioned. The campus paper announced a memorial service held in the chapel, but nothing more.

Trey maintained it was an accident. If it weren't for Will's confession, Claire wouldn't have known of Trey's involvement. Or doubted his innocence. Or gone to the extremes she did to protect me. I had distanced myself from my father's alcoholism knowing we didn't share genes. Now here was this suspect man whose genes I did share. How would I distance myself from him?

★ ★ ★

Lauren shared Godfrey's Homecoming Weekend schedule, which included a class parade, lobster bake, fun run, and special tours and performances. I wasn't sure I was going to show up until I found myself sneaking into the back of the Coffee House for the alumni performance of Looking for Treble. I recognized Trey among the eight men. My breath caught. He was taller in person and stylish in a button-down and dark jeans. His hair combed into place with product. Prosperous New York business-man versus my father, the high-school history teacher, with his sagging corduroy pants, mismatched socks, and cardigan sweaters patched at the elbows. Heat rushed to my face. I pressed back against the wall out of sight. On stage next to him was an aging boy scout, presumably Will, and sitting in a back booth with per-fectly styled dark hair, wearing a sheer black top over a camisole, skinny jeans, and resembling an actress who earned roles for characters younger than her actual age, had to be Sloan, chatting with some other couples. They all looked a decade younger than I had imagined. A generation after my parents.

Trey tapped the mike, smiled with a wattage that lit the room's corners and said, "After all these years, we're still Looking for Treble." He winked, blew the pitch pipe, and the men launched into song. They were good. Surprisingly good. I wished again I had inherited the singing gene. I could hold a tune all right and harmonize with the radio, but I never had any special talent. My mother often saying, "Well dear, I guess you take after me in the vocal category too."

The men shuffled around the stage singing and beatboxing hits from their college days. Will and Trey played off each other. Still the two strongest voices. The audience reacted as if they were sixteen-year-old girls at the latest boy-band concert. I felt myself being drawn to the stage.

Trey was soloing on "Stray Cat Strut" when he looked straight at me. His eyes narrowed, then widened. His smile faltered for a beat before he shook his head as if clearing his vision. Trey glanced over at Sloan, who hadn't missed his reaction. She cast a cool stare over the audience. I shrank back into the crowd.

I knew I should leave before they finished their set, but I didn't. I listened to the crowd murmur, the distant clanking sounds of the kitchen, and absorbed the collegiate vibe of the CoHo, imagining it back in the early nineties, the alumni who now packed the room thirty years younger. When they finished their set, I slipped into the frigid night air and hugged myself. The outside of the Coffee House was dimly lit by a streetlamp. I lurked in the shadows, arms crossed for warmth. Unsure. The door opened, silhouetting Trey in a sliver of light. The din of voices faded behind him as he stepped outside and shut the door. He stared at me. I didn't look away.

"I'm sorry," he said after an uncomfortable silence. "But you look so much like someone I knew."

"It's okay," I said. "I haven't quite accepted how much I look like her either."

Trey's brow furrowed. He took my elbow, glancing back over his shoulder at the closed door. "Walk with me."

He dropped my arm when I nodded. Trey headed away from the CoHo. I matched his strides, silent. We said nothing until we stepped inside the chapel sanctuary.

"Who are you?"

"Your daughter."

"You can't be," he said.

"She put me up for adoption."

"But she drowned."

"She didn't. She died in a car accident earlier this year. I found out from her lawyer."

"Where?"

"Here in Maine. She had a house on Lone Loon Pond."

He pressed his hands to his temples. "All these years?"

"Only the last ten. After her husband died of cancer in California, she came back."

"I don't know what to say." He raked his hands through his hair and sat down in the front pew.

"Let's start again," I said. "Hi, I'm Lindsay. You're my father."

"How did you find me?"

"She left a journal. Look," I said. "I have no expectations. I have a mother and father who love me. I never planned to find you."

"But now you have."

"Now I have."

"Sloan," he said. "I need to get back."

"Lauren knows how to reach me."

Trey nodded. He stood to leave and then turned back at the chapel door. "You're good?"

"I'm good," I said.

"That's good." He studied me before stepping out the door.

I collapsed on the pew and looked to the arched ceiling. The chapel felt cozy. Safe. Warm. I imagined it lit with jack-o-lanterns. Stretching out on the pew, I cradled my head in my hands and stared out the tall windows at the ominous shadows of branches reaching toward the glass like gnarled hands. The door of the chapel pushed open. I sat up, expecting to see Trey.

Sloan stood in the entryway. Intimidating in a long, camel-colored cashmere coat. She closed the heavy door behind her. I blew out my breath slowly and willed myself to channel Claire. She stared at me, taking in my features while I held still.

"What do you want?" Sloan asked, removing her gloves.

"Nothing from you."

"I don't believe you."

"It's true," I said.

She walked down the nave, touching the backs of the pews, then stopped and turned to face me. Staring me down like a prosecutor. "Claire was right to hide you. Does she know you're here?"

I watched Sloan. "No."

"Will you tell her?"

I shrugged.

"It's in everyone's best interest if you leave Trey alone. We have children."

"I'm afraid it's not your decision."

"Trey will do what I tell him."

I forced a short laugh.

"Stay away from my family." Sloan repeated her lawyer stare and turned to leave.

"I'm Lindsay, by the way," I said to her retreating form. "Nice to meet you, Sloan. You're exactly as my mother described." Sloan didn't look back.

When the heavy door shut behind her, I sank into the pew and regretted not believing in God.

★ ★ ★

The next evening, the sun had just dropped behind the mountains, and I was soldering a new jewelry piece in my dining-room studio when the doorbell chimed. Riley started barking. Trey stood on the front porch, his hands jammed into his pockets.

"Sorry to just barge in on you like this, but I figured I owed you one." He stepped inside, wiping his feet on the mat. He looked around the living room, taking in the bookshelves and fireplace, the prayer flags and the antique skis. Riley stayed behind me, watching.

"Surreal, huh?" I said.

"If I had known."

"She didn't want you to."

He paced the room. "It never felt right to me," he said. "Her drowning. But I can't even fathom that she was willing to do this. Was I that bad?"

"Why don't you have a seat," I said.

Trey slipped off his coat and sat in the armchair by the fireplace. Riley stayed glued to my leg.

I thought back to Claire's April journal entry.

"What would you have done if you had known?" I asked.

He drew his hand across his face, then leaned forward, resting his elbows on his knees. "That's the thing," Trey said. "I would have gone out to California with her. Started fresh, away from my family and everything they wanted me to do."

"Escape."

He nodded. "She didn't give me the chance."

I sat down in the chair across from him. "She was pregnant."

"That night," he said, "I never should have let her leave."

"You married Sloan and you manage a hedge fund."

"I'm a good father," Trey said. "I love my kids. I provide for my family."

I thought of all the family trips we'd taken. The sports teams my father coached. The embarrassment I'd felt when he bragged about me. The ways he spoiled me. All those things that loving fathers do for their children. "Claire made what she thought was the best choice for her, and for me," I paused.

"Does Sloan know you're here?"

He shook his head. Studied me. "You let her think Claire was alive."

"Guilty," I said.

He pressed his lips together. "I didn't tell her otherwise."

A laugh escaped me.

"Don't you have questions?" he said. "I know I do."

"I'd love to know my health history."

"Pretty clean on my side. Some alcoholism, poor eyesight, no major cancers. My grandmother had dementia, but my mother hasn't shown signs. My father died of a heart attack, but that was due to lifestyle choices. What about your parents?"

"Alive and well in California."

"I feel like I should thank them."

"Let's hold off on that."

Trey narrowed his eyes. "You haven't told them."

"Only about the house."

"Huh," he said. "Why not?"

"I don't know." I scratched Riley on the head. "They've always been open and supportive of me finding my birth parents . . ."

"But . . ."

"But, I need to know how I feel first."

"Fair enough," he said.

"Tell me about you and Claire."

Trey described how they met, the Christmas break they spent together, and that she smelled like vanilla and had a deep, unexpected laugh. How she loved to read and run. How devastated he felt when he lost her, and how he didn't have the energy to fight his parents, so he moved in with Sloan and went to work at his father's company as preordained.

I shared what I had learned from Lauren. Told him about growing up in California, going to Amherst, managing the private art collection, starting my own jewelry business. We talked late into the night.

It was nearly dawn when Trey left. We made no future plans. Wrapping a blanket around my shoulders, I made my way down to the dock, Riley at my heels. There was a familiarity about Trey, not in a fatherly way, but in the way when you first meet someone and there is an instant connection that makes you think you must have known them in a past life. I sat cross-legged on the grey weathered wood. Riley lay with his head cradled in my lap. I stroked his silky ear. The sunken town had been an asset to Claire. Lone Loon Pond a place of sanctuary. The golden sun rising over the dark silhouette of the mountains glowed on the mirrored surface, and the basin lit with the honey tones of dawn. The needles of the pines rimming the lake cast feathered shadows. Aside from the few lone docks, the entire area appeared remote and uninhabited. Except for a moose foraging in the reeds.

CHAPTER EIGHTEEN

Lindsay

Beverly stood on the front step facing the primeval garden, her elbows jutting from her hips. She whirled around when she heard the door. "Lindsay."

She squeezed my arms. I kept my hands in my pockets.

"It's just a shame the garden has gotten so out of control. I blame myself. I never realized how much work Claire put into it."

"I really appreciate you coming over. It's mostly clothes that we need to sort." Beverly followed me upstairs to the bedroom. She ran her hand along the curve of the bed's footboard, gently stroked the flannel comforter as if it were a fine piece of linen, then fingered the edge of a gilded-framed picture of Claire and Riley I'd reset on the dresser.

"You're welcome to take that," I said.

"Don't you want it?"

"Claire left me plenty. I want you to have it. Let's start a pile." I set the frame in an empty box. "How about I take the dresser, and you take the closet?"

Beverly straightened the pile of books on the nightstand.

I pulled open the top dresser drawer containing socks. "I figure we're sorting into Trash, Goodwill, and Keep." I scooped the socks into an empty box then added bras and underwear from the next two drawers. My cell phone vibrated on the top of the dresser. I sent my mother to voicemail.

"Don't not take that on my account," Beverly said.

"It can wait. How's the closet coming?" I pushed an empty box at her chest like a basketball pass and pulled open the next drawer. T-shirts. Hangers clicked behind me as Beverly flipped through Claire's clothes.

"Oh," Beverly sighed. The hanger slid on the rod. "Oh and this one." I glanced over my shoulder. Beverly held a dress up to her cheek.

"A good memory?"

"This was one of her favorites. She wore it on special occasions." It looked like a simple, but elegant little black dress that you could spruce up or down depending on the occasion. What you'd expect in any woman's closet.

"She'd twist her hair into a knot, showing off her regal neck and high cheekbones, and of course those eyes. Bright blue. She was beautiful, in a very natural way." Beverly looked at me. "She loved the theater. We'd drive down to Boston for the weekend, staying at the Parker House, then we'd go out to dinner in the North End and see whatever show was in town. She always wore this."

Beverly thrust the dress at me. "Try it on."

"Uh." I took a step backward.

"Please?"

I took the dress from her and stepped into the bathroom. When my mother had me try on her wedding dress, I knew it would fit before I held it up. I also knew I wasn't getting married anytime soon, and if I ever did, I wanted to pick my own dress, so I only tried it on to humor her. When my mother zipped it and I turned around, we both stared at my reflection in the mirror. It was as if the dress had been designed for me.

"It fits," I'd said.

"That sure brings back memories," my mother had said. She didn't have to say how much I resembled her young self. I'd seen the wedding picture on her dresser all my life. The dress went back into the box on the top shelf of the hall closet.

"Do you need me to zip it?" Beverly's voice came through the door.

"I got it," I said, awkwardly bending my arm behind my back. I adjusted the drape of the silky material around my waist. Like the wedding dress, I knew it would fit. Also like the wedding dress, I didn't plan on keeping it. I'd hoped the style would be too old for me, but it had a classic cut that flattered my body. Beverly tapped on the door.

"Oh!" she inhaled sharply and brought her hands up to her cheeks. She gathered my hair in her hands and twisted it up. "You're just as beautiful as your mother."

"Thank you," I mumbled.

"You have to keep it."

"Oh no," I said and reached around for the zipper.

"You must."

I held the door for her to leave the bathroom and forced a smile. "Why don't you see what else is in there?" I slipped off the dress and rehung it. When I came out of the bathroom, Beverly seemed to have started a Goodwill pile.

"I never did like this ratty college sweatshirt that she puttered around the house in." Beverly held up the familiar grey-and-purple logo and my stomach flipped.

"She didn't even go to Amherst."

"I did."

"Oh." She dropped it down to her side. "Do you want it?"

I shook my head. Riley was curled on the middle of the bedspread. Beverly reached out and patted his head. Riley lifted an eyebrow.

"When did Claire get Riley?" I asked.

"Six years ago? He found her. She was weeding when he came trotting through the open garden gate with a bone in his mouth. He looked around, found an unplanted patch of soil, dug—dirt clods flying everywhere—until he had a hole. He dropped in his bone, buried it back up, then trotted up the front steps and sat on the mat facing the door. She let him in and that was that. She loved that dog like a child." She glanced at me. "Sorry."

"It's okay. I'm starting to understand." My phone vibrated again. I groaned. My mother had already left a message saying she'd run into Emily at the grocery store and she was worried about me. I wasn't sure if she meant she was worried, or Emily. Since reading Claire's journal I had been dodging talking to both of them, not knowing what I wanted to say.

"Please, you can answer it."

"It's just my mother. I can talk to her later."

"She must be worried about you."

"She is, but it's really my father who is worried sick and constantly nagging her to call me."

"Why doesn't he just call you himself?" She placed a pair of dress pants in the Goodwill box.

"That's just not the way it works."

"I see," she said.

But I could see she didn't. I didn't blame her. I sighed. "You just have to know my family."

"I did." Beverly turned her back on me to take a shirt off its hanger. "I knew your mother," she said into the closet.

I stared at the spot between her shoulder blades. "Not the mother who raised me."

She turned and wagged her finger at me. "She's your mother just the same."

I stiffened. "Beverly, she may have given birth to me, and I thank her for that because I would have made a different choice, but my *parents* are the people who raised me."

"But you look like Claire, and you act like Claire."

"But I'm not Claire." I sank down on the bed and rubbed my forehead. "Nor do I want to be."

Beverly recoiled as if I'd slapped her. "But you're here, wearing her bracelet!"

"I *made* it. I don't know how she found it, maybe she saw it in the gallery on one of your trips to Boston."

"The Elizabeth Elliot Gallery?"

Goosebumps ran up my arms. "Yes. I worked there."

"Had she known, she would have told me." Beverly opened the jewelry box and lifted out a bracelet and then a necklace I'd designed, letting them run through her fingers like water.

I stood from the bed and came beside her. "You didn't know about me, did you?" I said quietly. "Until the lawyer told you."

She arranged the pieces on the dresser then lifted out the top jewelry tray revealing a stack of letters in the bottom of the box. My breath caught. It was the handwriting. The same loopy chicken scratch I knew as well as my own. I watched my hand reach out as if it belonged to someone else and take an envelope off the top of the pile. Beverly stared at me. The return address was as I feared. I went numb and leaned against the dresser. Riley stood up from the bed.

"There are others." Beverly reached into the jewelry box.

"Please don't touch them. Sorry. I just need to be alone right now." I grabbed the stack of letters and ushered her to the door. "Thank you for your help. I'll call you."

Beverly scrutinized me, then turned and walked down the stairs.

"Oh, Riley," I said burying my face in his neck. He was warm and soft and smelled like rosemary. "What has my mother been keeping from me?" I inhaled his sweet scent, drawing strength from him and slid my finger under the flap of the first envelope.

★ ★ ★

My mother picked up on the second ring. "Oh good. We were starting to get worried," she said. "How's Maine?"

"Mother, I found your letters." The silence stretched, filling the three thousand miles between us. I could picture her standing in her tennis outfit in her apple-themed kitchen. I wished I could see her face, but I knew it would be that perfect mask. "You wrote her about me," I said. "How *could* you and not tell me?"

"Well, Lindsay, I wasn't sure you'd want to know. You never asked about her. If you had, I would have told you."

"You told her all about me."

"She made a very difficult choice at a very young age. I thought she deserved to know how you turned out. Give her some peace of mind."

The leaves on the beech tree out the dormer window were thinner now, caught in the act of changing for the seasons like an actor between scenes. Claire's original letter to me had never left my parents' file. It hadn't needed to.

"You should have told me anyway." I threw the phone on the bed, grabbed my coat, and ran down the stairs and out the back door. Movement felt good. I turned down the wooded path, lengthened my stride, and sprinted to the end of the dock, coming to an abrupt halt at the water.

"How could she? How could she? How could she?" I stomped on the wooden slats, then sat cross-legged on the dock with my face buried in my hands. Riley licked my cheek.

★ ★ ★

Back at the house, I dropped into one of the Adirondack chairs on the front porch, cell phone pressed to my ear. My foot tapping.

"Slow down, Lindsay," Emily said. "You're talking too fast." And then muffled like she had her hand over the receiver, "Not now, Connor, Mommy's talking to Auntie Lindsay."

"I said, I found letters from my mother written to Claire."

"Where? Not now, Connor."

"In her jewelry box. They were all about me. Written every year on my birthday."

"Hold on a minute, Lindsay."

I stared at the garden. It was getting worse by the minute. As if the weeds were replicating themselves, mutating out of control.

Again Emily's voice was muffled, "Connor, what is it? No, you may not have another cookie before dinner." Then louder, "Okay, I'm back. Claire sent you a letter on your birthday?"

"No, not me, my—"

"Hold on again. Connor, how many cookies your sister's had should not concern you. Mommy said you may not have another one."

"Look, obviously this isn't a good time for you."

"No, it's fine," Emily said. "You'll understand when you have kids."

I closed my eyes in a slow blink, then pinched the bridge of my nose. Emily called my name as I pressed the button to end the call.

My feet slid into Claire's gardening clogs. I found work gloves in the shed, stiff from disuse but they loosened as I flexed my fingers. I dragged a tarp behind me. The gate needed a good shove, the bottom entangled in weeds, but the hinges moved smoothly once freed. The garden covered the size of my entire Southwestern Jail lot back in California.

Wood chip pathways meandered among the beds. Plants were arranged for contrasting, yet fluid colors. A weathered bench hid in a private corner. Centered in another cove sat a table with two chairs. The dense hum of bees pollinating the flowers filled the air. At a different time, I could see how peaceful this garden would make me feel. I kicked the gate closed and snapped the tarp onto the ground.

I tossed the trowel aside and half dove into the first patch of greenery, tearing and yanking vegetation with my gloved hands, barely discriminating between invasive weeds and nurtured plants. Grabbing them two, three, at a time, I leaned my weight back to pull against the more stubborn roots, which made a satisfying ripping sound. No match for my outrage. Riley began digging. Rich black soil sprayed as he disappeared into a deepening hole.

I yanked weeds by their tops, whacked the roots on the ground to dislodge the dirt, and pitched them in the direction of the tarp. My arms started to ache. A bead of sweat rolled from my forehead down my nose despite the cool weather. Something wicked pricked my finger through the glove, undoubtedly drawing blood. I raked my fingers through the dark earth and then plunged forward into the soil, spread-eagle, and pressed my cheek into the dampness. I lay still and listened to the cadence of my own breathing. The ground smelled rich and earthy, like a living organism. It drew the indignation from my body. My mother said she would have told me if I had asked.

When I'd mostly regained myself, I squatted back on my heels to survey my work. The fresh-turned soil looked clean, but I knew it would not stay that way. Riley trotted past with what looked like a carrot in his mouth. He cocked his head at me, and then flopped down with whatever it was between his front paws and wolfed it down in three bites. I dragged a bag of mulch over from the shed and tucked it around the plants. When I was done, one bed looked cared for, but it made the rest of the garden seem even wilder.

"You've been busy." I heard Beverly over my shoulder. I imagined what I must look like. Covered in dirt. Knees damp from kneeling in the soil. Hair every which way. "I came over to check on you."

"Thanks."

Beverly looked wrought, as if she'd been crying. "Why would Claire keep anything from me?"

"It wasn't about you. Come inside. I'll make you some tea and you can read the letters."

Beverly sat at the kitchen island sipping Darjeeling, reading. "These must have hurt Claire. All the things they did for you, that Claire couldn't."

I leaned against the counter. "It's just my life. It wasn't meant spitefully." My cell rang.

"Hello there." Lucas's voice was almost musical. "I've been thinking about you."

"Do you mind if I take this?" I asked Beverly, stepping into the other room. I took a deep breath and said to Lucas, "So, my mother was writing letters about me to Claire without telling me."

Silence. "You know what I do when I'm upset?" he said. "Chop wood."

"I took it out on the garden."

"Then for the garden's sake, I guess I better come over and teach you how to chop wood."

★ ★ ★

I loved the heaviness of the ax as I hefted it over my head. The clean way it sliced through the log like kindling. "You're a natural," Lucas said. "Are you sure you've never done this before?"

"Heard of Duraflame? When I was looking at houses to buy, it was hard to find ones that had fireplaces and that was on my must-have list."

"I guess you could always put one in."

"Not in California. If the house doesn't already have a fireplace, you can't add one. Air quality."

"Did you find a house?"

"Yeah, actually my realtor found the perfect little place for me."

"You bought it?"

"No," I paused. Bit my cheek. "I didn't."

Lucas followed me into the house. I kicked off the garden clogs in the entryway and glanced in the hall mirror. Dirt streaked my face like war paint. Leaves entangled my hair. "I'm filthy."

"I think it's kind of sexy," Lucas said.

"What I could use right now is a bubble bath."

"Sounds good to me." Lucas stripped off his shirt and threw it at my feet. I only hesitated a moment before following him upstairs.

We soaked at opposite ends of the candlelit tub, vanilla-scented bubbles touching our chins. Lucas took my foot in his hand to massage my arch. Riley trotted up to the side, poked his nose at a bubble, and snorted. Standing on hind legs, he hooked his front paws over the edge as if testing the water.

"Riley, no!" I said. He looked at me as if he didn't understand the problem. "A little privacy please." He dropped back down, turned in three circles, and curled up on the bathmat with his back to us.

★ ★ ★

In the fog of the morning, Riley snoring from his dog bed perplexed me, until I realized it was Lucas who spooned the length of my spine. I snuggled deeper into the flannel sheets, savoring the coziness of the early hour, until it was interrupted by car tires crunching on the gravel driveway.

"Are you expecting someone?" Lucas asked. He propped himself on his elbow and glanced out the dormer window.

"No. What time is it?" I went to the window and didn't recognize the car. It stopped and the driver's door opened. "Crap!"

"What?"

"It's my mother. Put some clothes on!" I shoved Lucas's jeans at him. My mother stood outside the car with her hands on her hips studying the house. Even though I knew she couldn't see inside, I felt as if she were looking through the walls right at us. I threw on clothes and bounded down to the door. Lucas's shirt lay in the entry hall. I balled it and threw it up the stairs.

Gripping the doorknob, I rested my forehead on the door, and allowed myself a moment to appreciate the cool wood pressed against my skin. I took three deep breaths and then stepped outside, pulling the door shut behind me.

"Mother, what a surprise." I stood on the porch, arms folded tightly across my chest. And not because I wasn't wearing a bra.

"You didn't give me much choice."

"How'd you find me?"

"Remember, dear? I knew the address. I took a redeye last night." She looked up at the house. "It's bigger than I imagined."

"Welcome to Maine, the way life should be."

"Let me just get my bag out of the trunk."

I made no attempt to help as she lugged out her suitcase and rolled it unsteadily up the gravel driveway. She stopped at the garden gate.

"Claire often wrote about her garden," she said. "It looks like it could use some work."

"How often did you write?"

"It started out on your birthday, but when we switched to email it became more often."

"How often?"

"A couple times a year."

"Twice?"

She tipped her head back and forth. "Four times. It wasn't always about you, Lindsay. We became friends."

"Well, bully for you," I said, then cringed. It was exactly what she would have said.

"Are you going to invite me in?"

"By all means, Mother." I held the door for her. "Please come in."

She set her suitcase on the bench in the entry and hung her coat on the hook. Riley ran out of the kitchen and sniffed her legs. "This must be Riley." She patted his head. We heard a thump.

"Is someone else here?"

"My friend Lucas," I said to her.

"Lucas?" I called up the stairs.

"In here," Lucas's voice came from the kitchen. "You're just in time for breakfast."

She stepped through the kitchen doorway. "A handsome young man who makes breakfast? Isn't that refreshing."

"Mother."

"Bacon and eggs?" Lucas asked.

"That sounds lovely," my mother said. "Now how do you two know each other?"

"Lucas was family friends with Claire. He took care of Riley until I got here. We met the first time I came to Maine."

"First time?" She glanced at me over the rim of her teacup.

"Perhaps I should let you two catch up," Lucas said.

"That's not necessary.

My mother slipped into her full-social mode. "Now tell me about yourself Lucas . . ."

I watched as they flirted, both at their most charming. Under different circumstances it would have pleased me to see my mother getting along with my boyfriend, but Lucas wasn't my boyfriend, and I wasn't so sure right then that she was really my mother.

Lucas looked at his phone. "This has been fun, ladies, but I better hit the road."

"Can't you blow off work and spend the day with us?"

"Now Lindsay, he has already cooked us breakfast. Let him

get on with his day." My mother stood and started putting dishes in the washer.

"Are you sure?" I asked, wringing my napkin. "There's plenty to do around here."

"I'll text you later," he said.

Riley followed him to the door and I followed Riley, who nosed me in the leg, urging me to go with Lucas. I held myself back, gripping the door with one hand and Riley's collar with the other. I watched until his truck turned out of the long driveway. I thought about shutting my mother inside and taking Riley for a long walk around the lake, but that would just prolong the inevitable. I squatted down to Riley's eye level and took his face in my hands. He tried to lick my nose. "Riley, give me the power to get through this." I kissed him, stood, and returned to the kitchen.

"What a charming young man," my mother said, her back to me doing dishes. She turned around and caught my eye. "And how convenient he was able to come over for breakfast."

"Yes," I said. "How convenient." I crossed my arms. "If you want to help sort through the house, that's fine, but don't expect me to entertain you."

"Aren't you going to give me the grand tour?"

"Maybe Riley will."

My mother's shoes sounded like a woodpecker on the hard maple floor as she moved from room to room downstairs. I darted upstairs to straighten the ransacked bed before she confirmed her suspicions.

Beverly and I had made a fair dent in the bedroom before the letter incident. The dresser was completely empty. The closet only held a pair of hand-knit wool sweaters, a few nice dresses, and a limited number of shoes stored in their boxes. Claire's shoes were too small for Beverly, but I thought she might want the sweaters, so I placed them in the box along with the picture and added the other pictures on top for good measure. I kept the jewelry box.

For all practical purposes, the bedroom now looked like a room at an inn. It had knickknacks, books, magazines, and pictures on the wall, but empty drawers and a spacious closet waiting for my things.

My mother and Riley were nowhere to be found until I saw them at the end of the dock. My mother didn't particularly like animals. She let Daniel sit on her lap when she read, the corduroy worn from him kneading her thighs, but she didn't necessarily pet him. Now, Riley sat at her feet, ears perked toward her. My mother hid a stick behind her back. Riley was trying to sit still, but his body squirmed with an energy he couldn't contain, like a spring about to uncoil.

My mother flung the stick into the water, following through like she was hitting a tennis forehand. Riley exploded, his toenails digging into the dock, and dove after the stick. Riley saw me first. He climbed the bank, shook lake water onto my mother, and then he trotted past her to me. "Good boy," I said.

My mother wiped at her pant legs. "Pretty view."

"If you don't look too closely."

"It's so different from Tahoe. The landscape is not nearly as dramatic, yet it has an almost magical, timeless, feel." She had articulated what I felt. I started to soften, but then caught myself. We both turned and followed Riley back to the house. Riley held his feet up one by one to be dried while my mother sat on a kitchen stool watching our routine. "He really responds to you, doesn't he?" she said.

"Mother," I sighed. "Why are you here?"

"To support you."

"Don't you mean to do damage control? Don't worry, I'm three thousand miles away from anyone you know. I won't reflect badly on you."

"Have you talked to Emily? She was concerned about you."

"I haven't gotten to it." I tossed the dog towel toward the top of the washing machine but missed. It slid down the side. I tried to fit my arm between the machines, but I couldn't quite reach the corner of the towel.

"You really should call her. It's the right thing to do."

"The right thing to do?" I spun around and forgot about the towel.

"How could you tell *her* about me, and not tell me about *her*?"

"Lindsay, I didn't want to upset you. It would have been different if you had been curious about her over the years, but you never seemed interested. Your father—"

"My father?" I cut her off. "Now there's a great example of someone you always put before me."

"Lower your voice."

I stormed out of the kitchen and up to the bedroom with Riley at my heels. Yanking open the shower door, I turned on the water, stripped off my clothes, and stepped inside. The hot spray burned my bare skin for an instant and then began to soothe. I sat in the center of the shower with my knees pulled up to my chest. Why hadn't I been curious? What had I lost without even knowing it? Who was I really mad at? Did I want to find the town under the lake?

The water poured over my head and down the drain, slowly taking my anger with it as my fingers pruned. Riley pressed his nose against the shower door and licked the glass at my face level.

★ ★ ★

I dried myself with a thick towel, wrapping it around me like a cocoon. Pulling a comb through my hair, I stepped over to the window and opened it to let the shower steam escape and the cool air fill the bathroom. My mother was in the garden weeding one of the beds I had yet to attack. She looked frailer than I remembered. Her clothes were a little larger. Her body slightly smaller. Her shoulders more rounded. A big straw hat shielded her face from the sun. I picked up my discarded clothes and was halfway into my jeans when I heard Beverly's voice from the window.

"Who do you think you are?"

I scooted down the stairs barefoot.

Beverly stood with one hand on her hip and shook her finger at my mother. "How dare you enter this garden."

My mother stood up from her weeding. "I'm sorry, have we met?"

She brushed her garden-gloved hands together to wipe off the excess dirt.

"I know who you are." Beverly's eyes narrowed to slits.

"Beverly," I said. "Please."

"Stay out of this, Lindsay." Beverly held her hand to my face like a traffic cop.

My mother put her hands on her hips. "I'll request you don't use that tone of voice with my daughter."

"Mother, please."

"She's Claire's daughter."

I tried to step between them, but Beverly moved around me and blocked our path to the garden gate.

"I beg to differ." My mother gripped the garden trowel in her hand tighter.

"You kept Claire from her."

"I did no such thing."

"You wrote horrible things to her to make Claire feel inadequate as a mother."

My mother's face went pale. "What are you talking about?"

"Lindsay let me read the letters."

"That's preposterous. Those letters were nothing of the sort. Lindsay, who is this?"

"I live next door." Beverly waved her hand in the direction of her house. "I was Claire's best friend. We shared everything."

"Except she never mentioned she'd had a child, let alone that she was in contact with my mother," I said.

"Claire was your mother."

"My *birth* mother." I threw up my hands in the air. "Grace, the woman standing in front of you, is my mother. Claire is gone. You need to accept that and get a grip on yourself. Do you think she would have wanted you to act like this?"

Beverly sank down onto the garden bench. "I thought I knew her," she whispered.

"You did know her," I said more gently. "But you can never know everything about a person."

My mother sat on the bench next to Beverly. "Was there a ceremony?" I was stopped cold. To my mother Claire was a person. A pen pal. A friend. It hadn't occurred to me that she was buried somewhere. That there was a physical presence, not just a house and a dog and the material remains of a woman I didn't know. Was she scattered in the garden? Buried under the beech tree? Deep-sixed in the lake? Was her ghost trapped between worlds, not knowing she had been killed in the accident?

"Yes," Beverly nodded with a sniff. "It was lovely. The whole town came out for a celebration of her life. So many people loved her. She wanted to be buried next to her husband," Beverly continued. "They're in California. I wish it were closer so I could keep fresh flowers on her grave. She would love that."

I pictured two plots on a golden hill under a sprawling oak tree in the Bay Area foothills.

My mother squeezed Beverly's hand. "It must be hard without her."

Beverly sighed. "I keep finding myself picking up the phone to call her, or halfway out the door to come over before I realize she's gone."

Both women sat quietly for a moment, staring into the garden. The bees hummed.

"Claire wrote me first," my mother broke the silence. "Her husband had just died. She was completely lost. That letter terrified me. I knew I was being irrational, but I was afraid I'd somehow lose Lindsay. I almost didn't respond, but then I realized that I had a responsibility."

Yes, you had a responsibility, I thought. *To me.*

"That was before I met her," said Beverly.

My mother nodded. "She moved to Maine shortly thereafter and when Lindsay's birthday came around the next year, I found Claire weighing heavily on my mind for the first time since we brought Lindsay home from the hospital wrapped in that little pink blanket. I wrote Claire and she wrote me back."

"Why didn't you tell me?" I asked.

"Adoption is a tricky thing, Lindsay, and the law protects the child. At the time she gave you up, she relinquished her rights as your mother. I told myself if you asked about her, I'd tell you everything, but then you didn't and over time we built our own relationship. Maybe not telling you was wrong."

"But you did tell Claire about Lindsay," Beverly said.

"Of course. Lindsay was her child. She gave me a gift and as much as I feared losing my daughter, I knew how much I had to lose. At the time Claire made the decision, she had no idea what she was giving up."

"Did she want to meet me?" I asked.

"I think she was afraid," my mother said.

"But she kept track of me. She went to my gallery. She bought my jewelry."

"I didn't know that," my mother said. "But it makes sense, I sent her the information. I wonder if you met her."

My shoulders tensed.

"No," Beverly said. "I would have remembered. I was always

with Claire on those trips. They were our special time together."
My mother raised an eyebrow at me over Beverly's head. "She
didn't tell you about me?"

My mother patted Beverly's knee. "I'm sure she did and I just
don't remember. I'm not as sharp as I used to be." We watched
Beverly disappear into the trees that separated the houses. My
mother turned to me. "She's an odd duck."

"I know. I'm not quite sure why Claire was such good
friends with her, or maybe she really wasn't." I shrugged.

"Grief does strange things to people," my mother said.

I dug my bare toe into the soil. "I kind of think Beverly wants
me to be Claire."

"Give her time." My mother stood from the bench and pulled
her gardening gloves back on. "Claire wasn't one to suffer fools.
Beverly might surprise you." She knelt back down to the bed
she had been weeding before being interrupted by Beverly, then
turned to look at me. "Should I have told you about Claire?"

I squatted down next to her, reaching to touch a flower. If
I pulled off the petals one by one would I have an answer? "I
don't know," I said. "But you're right about one thing, it never
occurred to me to ask."

She nodded and dug her trowel into the soil.

★ ★ ★

I spent the better part of the next week with my mother gardening, now able to distinguish flowering weeds from nurtured
plants. My back hurt from bending. My knees became imprinted
with tiny rocks. I'd finally flushed the dirt from under my finger-
nails by soaking in the bubble bath and using a small brush. After
waking with a crick in my neck and barely being able to bend
over to pick the shampoo bottle off the shower floor, I booked an
appointment with the local massage therapist.

As I lay belly down on the massage table, the universal spa

scent of eucalyptus and lavender infused the air and Andean pan-flute music floated in the background, reminding me of my wish. Outside the room, a wiry woman whose name I'd already forgotten waited for me to settle. There was a soft knock, then the whoosh of a door. "Are you comfortable?" She adjusted the sheet.

"Yes, thank you." I sighed in anticipation. The massage therapist rubbed her hands together, inhaled deeply, and then leaned her weight into the heels of her palms as she kneaded the length of my spine. This morning while I sipped my latte and listened to my podcast at a little table hidden along a twisted path, I'd noticed Riley gnawing another carrot. "Where did you get that?"

He followed me to the vegetable section where enough beets, cauliflower, and kale ripened that if I didn't act, they would go to waste. He wrapped his lips around a leafy green sprout emerging from the soil, and gave it a quick yank. Out popped a carrot. "You little devil." The fence around the garden was not just to keep out deer.

"My, you have a lot going on in here," the massage therapist said.

"I've been weeding the garden."

"This is more than gardening." She worked down my hamstrings, smoothing the muscles and kneading out the pebble-like knots. Every time she pressed a sensitive spot, instead of tensing, I tried to relax deeper. I slipped into a trance. I could hear the soft music, smell the lavender lotion and feel the pressure of fingers, yet I floated a little outside of myself, as if in a dream, but one that I controlled. Her fist drilled into the bound muscles of my hip like a hot poker. I jerked back into my body. "This is a common spot of emotional pain," she said.

"Are you sure that's not just my IT band? I've always had tight hips."

"Something is causing this," she dug deeper. "Or someone."

"I recently broke up with my long-term boyfriend."

"This is unresolved."

My body tensed. The massage table creaked and shifted as the therapist placed her weight on it for better leverage. Her elbow bored into the hollow of my hip. I bit the padded table. "This is most likely something you've been carrying since childhood. Does that sound reasonable?"

I was silent. The massage therapist moved her elbow from my right hip to my left one. "Wow, this one is just as bad," she said. "Are you in therapy?"

"I'm *here*," I said.

★ ★ ★

My mother settled herself into one of the kitchen chairs, and I placed a cup of green tea in front of her. She dipped her tea bag into the mug. "What are your plans for Thanksgiving? We're going to Argentina and I was hoping you could house-sit." She flipped her hand. "If Daniel is still with us then."

I rolled my eyes. "I don't know where I'll be." I poured myself a mug of hot water from the kettle, opened a tea bag, and sat at the table across from her. Taking a deep breath I said, "So, I met my birth father, Trey."

My mother stopped dipping her tea bag.

"Did Claire ever tell you why she gave me up for adoption?"

She shook her head. "I never felt it was my place to ask."

"I swear, Mother," I said. "Apparently she thought she was protecting me from Trey's family."

"Was she?"

"I'm not sure I'll ever know."

My mother looked past me, out the window. "When you were younger, and so upset with your father all the time, I wondered if you'd go looking for him."

I shook my head. "It's not like I didn't have a father. Or that he didn't want to have a relationship with me. If he had tried as hard to quit drinking as he did to be a part of my life, we might be in a different place right now."

Maybe as a reaction to not giving me the one thing I wanted, my father could never say no to me about anything else as a child, causing me to have to decide what was considered excessive to protect us both from my mother. Back then, when he believed exercise to be something more than watching sports on television, I tied a rope through his back belt loop and let him pull me like a water-skier on my roller-blades when he jogged. He would start out strong, trotting down the driveway at a good clip, arms pumping with his stride, pulling me easily behind him. I just had to remember to keep my knees bent to absorb the bumps in the asphalt. A few blocks later he would slow to a walk and I would skate beside him, falling into an easy rhythm. When we approached the house of a neighbor we knew, my father would speed up to an Olympic pace, towing me behind him like a caboose until well past, where he would then bend over gasping for air until the eggplant color of his face returned to a solid tomato.

Sometimes for no reason he took me to McDonalds in the middle of the afternoon when it was sure to spoil both our dinners. Inevitably he'd say, "Don't tell Mom." And I wouldn't.

She blew on her tea and then took a tentative sip. "Your personalities were always so at odds, his anxious neediness against your stubborn demand for independence."

"Mom, it was more than that. I couldn't control his drinking, but I could remove myself from the situation. If he wanted to drink, I didn't have to be around it. But you wouldn't let that happen. And you undermined me."

"I did nothing of the sort."

"The only thing I could withhold from him was being a part of my life, but you made sure he was there every step of the way, even to the detriment of our own relationship."

"He's your father. Of course he wanted to be involved. He loves you."

"I know that, but it felt like you were always favoring him over me. Like my feelings came secondary. I struggled with trying to please you without compromising too much of myself."

"I don't know what to say, Lindsay. I just wanted us to be a family."

I took a deep breath and slowly exhaled it. "I'm starting to see that now." I felt for Riley under the table with my toe. "Mother, we need to try to change our dynamic. You can no longer put yourself between me and Dad."

She fished her tea bag out of her mug with her spoon and used the string to squeeze the liquid back into the cup.

"And I have to stop putting you there." I said.

She looked at me.

"Believe me, I'm not exactly excited about it either."

"It hasn't been that bad," she said.

I held up my hand. "Mother."

She shoulders dropped. "Okay. I'll try."

"Thank you."

My mother sipped her green tea. "So what do you think you're going to do about all this?" She gestured around the kitchen. "We didn't mean to complicate things by buying the other house."

"You meant well. You always mean well. That's what makes it so hard. It's not lost on me what a privileged position I'm in. But I feel like if I stay here, I'm disappointing you and Dad and if I go home, I'm disappointing Claire."

"I was always afraid of who you might find if you went looking for your birth parents. People don't give up children for adoption without good reason, but I was still prepared to help you. After I got to know Claire, I was relieved. I realized it would have been okay if you found her." She looked down into her tea cup and then back up at me. "I worry that if Claire didn't trust your birth father's family, she must have had good reason."

"She certainly felt she did, but I'm an adult now." I stood up and went to look out the window. "And only Trey's mother is alive."

"You've always made good choices," my mother said. "Your father and I were lucky in that regard."

I turned back to face her. "Part of me wishes that I could just go back to the way things were, but I can't pretend I don't know what I know."

"If you want to get to know your birth father, Dad and I will support you. That hasn't changed."

"I appreciate—"

Riley barked, startling me, then jumped to his feet, tail wagging, and went and stood at the back door to the kitchen. I glanced out the window. Beverly was approaching from the garden path. I let Riley out to greet her.

Beverly stuck her head inside the door, a tentative smile on her face. "I came with a peace offering," she said, presenting us with a coffee cake. "I'm sorry for how I acted the other day in the garden." She stepped into the kitchen.

My mother, ever the diplomat, shook her head. "It's already forgotten. Please come join us."

Beverly looked to me. "Yes," I said, only hesitating slightly. "I'll make you some tea." I went to the stove to reheat the kettle and pulled another mug out of the cabinet. Riley resettled under the table.

"Shall we have some of this delicious-looking cake?" my mother asked. I brought her a knife and set of small plates. She cut and plated a slice of coffee cake, sliding it to Beverly, while I placed a mug of tea in front of her and took my seat.

Beverly looked at the slice of coffee cake, the tea cup, and then at both of us. "I'm sorry. It's just been so lonely without

Claire." She frowned. "And you were right, Lindsay. I didn't know Claire had given up a child—you—for adoption. I can understand her not telling me. The woman I knew always looked forward, not back. But when I saw you, and you were so much like Claire, I don't know what came over me. I guess I just missed her."

"Grief is a funny thing," my mother said. She took a bite of cake. "This is delicious."

Beverly sliced off the tip of her coffee cake, but set her fork back down without eating. "When I found out that Claire'd been secretly buying your jewelry and in touch with you, Grace, it hurt and it made me question our friendship. I don't have a lot of female friends. My daughter says I might have been overinvested in my relationship with Claire." Beverly rolled her eyes. "You know how daughters can be," she said to my mother.

"That I do." My mother smiled.

Beverly picked up her fork again and put the bite of cake into her mouth. "Anyway," she said, washing it down with a sip of tea, "that's a long way of saying I'm sorry and that I hope we can start over."

"Where does your daughter live?" My mother asked, and while they started chitchatting, I thought about Claire's journal. Something about the way Claire had entrusted it with Lauren, never asking for it back, told me it was meant for my eyes only. One thing that had been clear reading it was that Claire did exactly what she wanted. Was that because she had no one to answer to but herself, or had she always been that way? Did my independence come from her, or from the security that my mother would always hold our family together? What was my nature, and what was my nurture? Trying to change our long-standing family-communication dynamic would be hard enough. Did I want to open the door to another potentially troubled relationship with Trey?

When Beverly left my mother said, "See, you should always give people a second chance."

"Does that apply to Trey as well?"

"I was thinking more about your father."

"More like chance number eight thousand, two hundred and forty-two for him." I cleared the remaining coffee cake from the table and wrapped it in plastic, then I sat back down at the table with her. "Mom, it's been really nice having you here helping me with the garden. I know what a big deal it was for you to come alone and I appreciate it. I'm glad you're here."

"It's been nice to spend mother/daughter time," she said. "I hope we can do it more often. Even go on another trip together."

"I'd like that," I said. "But you're still the one who's going to have to tell Dad."

She pursed her lips. "Maybe I'll start slipping antianxiety medication into his coffee."

I laughed. "I won't tell."

CHAPTER NINETEEN

Lindsay

Alone in the house after putting my mother back on a plane to California and unable to sleep, I called Emily. "You have my full attention," she said. I updated her, and right before hanging up she told me, "I miss you and I support you in whatever you decide, but you have to decide something."

I pulled up the online listing for the cottage with the red door and flipped through the photos, mapping out on my sketchpad how I would arrange my furniture in the new house. I saved the converted garage for last. It had been my dream to have a dedicated studio for my jewelry business—a creative space where I could immerse myself in my craft—and here one was. When I finished sketching but still felt wide awake, I shut my computer and pulled on a coat. My movement stirred Riley from his bed. He stretched and met me at the door.

The night sky was full of stars, and the moon so bright I didn't need a flashlight. We stepped off the front porch together and made our way to the garden. The occasional odd firefly still flickering along the walkway. The gate swung easily now. I held it open for Riley, closing it behind us. I followed the garden pathway as if walking a labyrinth. With each deliberate step, I slowed my breathing. Stilled my mind. Focused on finding clarity.

The garden overflowed with flowers and vegetables, the beds now weeded by me and my mother. I feared if I were to return to California it would once again revert back to its primal state. I cupped a handful of soil in my palms and brought it to my nose, smelling the earth, damp and alive, before letting the dirt trickle to the ground through my fingers, one clod at a time. I settled on the cushioned bench, tucking my legs underneath me. Riley sat in front of me and I half scratched, half massaged the length of his spine. Both of us taking comfort in the touch. I stared up at the moon as I had in Machu Picchu. The Incan Gods owed me an answer.

★ ★ ★

Lucas found me the next morning standing on the end of the dock throwing rocks into the lake while an eagle watched from high in a pine tree. The rocks made a satisfying plunking sound. Concentric circles flowed out from the spot where they disappeared under the surface. Riley lay next to me, his chin cradled in his front paws.

"There you are." Lucas rubbed his hands together. "Aren't you cold?"

"No." I threw another rock, trying to hit the exact spot where the last one disappeared.

"This lake will be frozen solid soon."

"What about the town?" I asked, my back to Lucas.

"Everyone up here is used to winter. We just put a few more layers on and go about our business. I suppose to a California girl like you—" He started to wrap his arms around me from behind.

"I meant the town under the lake," I interrupted.

He stopped short of hugging me and placed his hands on my shoulders. "Lindsay, there is no town under the lake."

I heaved the rock in my hand. "They couldn't have moved everything."

"Everything that mattered." Lucas took a rock from me and skipped it across the surface.

"When I was in Peru," I said. "I wished on a stone and placed it at the highest point of our hike. An Incan tradition."

"What did you wish for?"

"Clarity."

Lucas side-armed a rock, which made three hops before submerging. "And?"

"What's the opposite of clarity?"

"Turbidity. If you're talking water quality."

"Turbidity." I looked across the placid surface of Lone Loon Pond. Not a ripple of the town hidden underneath. Cormorants perched on nearby rocks holding their wings out from their bodies to dry, looking as if they were being accused of something.

"Do you want kids?"

"Of course," he said. "Don't you?"

"Call me selfish, but I like my life the way it is."

"Your biological clock just hasn't started ticking yet."

I threw a rock as hard as I could. "You know, everyone says that, but not everybody wants kids, or should have them."

I tried to imagine us living together in the farmhouse. Our two children chasing each other around the kitchen island and across the backyard to the dock. Cooking homegrown vegetables. Stealing moments during nap times to design jewelry. Hosting holidays in Maine. My parents joining Lucas's around a long dining table set with festive holiday dishware. Riley sleeping between us in the feather bed. Riley I could picture. The bed too, but with Riley's head on his pillow and mine on my own.

"If you want to get married and have babies and live a happy little life in Maine, I'm not the woman for you."

"Look," Lucas said. "I really enjoy spending time with you. I just want to get to know you better. We don't need to plan out our lives."

"Remember when I said I'd found a house in California? What I didn't tell you was my parents bought it for me."

"When?"

"Does it really matter?"

"So what you're really saying is, you're not going to give us a chance."

"All I'm saying is, I'm not going to change my mind about children."

★ ★ ★

When Lucas left, I sat on the end of the dock dangling my sandaled feet into the water, which tinted them a faint green. Beneath my toes, rocks and fallen trees rested on the mucky bottom, a crisscross of mossy branches at least twenty feet below, yet clearly visible as if I could reach down and touch them. It would be easy to believe a town never flourished in this valley. Its only inhabitants always moose, loons, mergansers, and the occasional eagle and osprey. Seeing all the way to the substratum of the pond from where I sat reassured me.

I pulled off my sweatshirt and emptied my shorts pockets. I stretched my toes toward the bottom, steeled myself against the cold and eased myself into the water. Riley paused to watch me, but he returned to gnawing his stick when I started treading water. I let the lake level come to just below my chin. The water kissed my lips. From this vantage point, the surface looked like a slate-blue plane. So serene and blissful that I didn't need to do anything but float with the sun on my upturned face, unafraid of the unknown secrets hidden beneath.

Lone Loon Pond was a man-made lake intended to bring an improved quality of life to the community. But did it? And at what cost?

I took a deep breath and sank under the surface. The water was still. The visibility that of an algae-filled swimming pool. I tried not to worry about leeches, or piranhas, or the Loch

Ness monster. I started swimming, slow and steady, to where the sunken town was rumored to have thrived. The bottom dropped away from me, boulders and tree trunks receding into the depths. When all I could see below me was empty space, I dove down, chasing what I thought might be waiting on the bottom, but had to resurface to breathe after only a few meters.

Treading water, I looked back to the dock. Riley stood alert at the end, watching me. I waved at him. "I'm okay," I said. "Sit tight."

Taking one last deep breath, I dropped back below the surface's illusion of serenity. Underwater again, I turned a full, slow circle looking in every direction, but the town and its secrets remained elusive. Outside of my vision and reach. There *was* one person I could go to for answers. I resurfaced and swam back to the dock. Riley's tail thumped on the wood.

Dry and back in the farmhouse, I started and deleted several polite texts to Trey, finally jumping in and telling him about my mother's relationship with Claire.

I'm in town next week for a mtg of the Board of Trustees at Godfrey, Trey replied. *Dinner?*

I thumbs-upped his text.

★ ★ ★

I stood in the parking lot staring at the restaurant. Although I had only visited in Claire's journal, there was no mistaking the location of her last meal with the Prices. It was a pale-yellow clapboard farmhouse, cozy and inviting. A restaurant that would appeal to me if there were not so much history attached. I was sitting on the bench on the front porch when Trey pulled up.

"Interesting choice," I said after greeting him.

"You don't like it?"

"The site of the last supper?"

He grimaced. "There are only a few restaurants in town, and this is my favorite. I've been coming here for years. Is it okay if we eat here?"

"Works for me."

Trey held the door and followed me inside. Once we'd been seated at a table tucked into a private corner near the fireplace, we studied each other.

"Do your parents know you're here?

"Does Sloan?"

We both opened our menus. "So," I said once we'd ordered, "I didn't get the singing gene."

He laughed. "My kids didn't either."

"But I'm athletic."

"What sports?"

"Soccer and horses mainly. I have to be outside. I don't know if that's growing up in California, or what."

"I'm the same way. Claire was too. That's why I wanted to be an environmental scientist. To have a career that kept me out in nature."

"But you didn't."

"No. My father," he started and stopped. Took a sip of water. "There were consequences to disobeying."

"How bad was it?"

Trey shook his head. "I've had a lot of therapy, and it's still hard to talk about. I worry that it's in me," he said. "When I get mad, it's all I can do to not . . ." Trey's voice trailed off.

I pictured the library clock tower at Godfrey. "My father's an alcoholic," I said. "But there's not a mean bone in his body. He smothers me out of love and fear that some harm will come to me. It's his drinking that's done the damage to our relationship."

"Consider yourself lucky."

"I do," I said.

When the waiter delivered our plates, Trey picked up his silverware, his fork hovering over his filet. "I read an article," he said, "about kids who are adopted having genealogical bewilderment. That normal psychological development requires knowledge of your identity and heredity, and children who don't have that feel separation, loss, and abandonment."

"I don't feel that way." I turned my plate so that my salmon was closest to me. "I have a very strong sense of self because I *don't* know my history. I am only related to me."

"Well, I *am* your biological father."

I wound my necklace around my finger. "My mother always talks about her ancestors as if they are mine, and I am the grandchild most like my grandfather. I'm interested in my grandparents, but that's where it stops. Any relative whom I'd never met might as well have been a historical figure for all the connection I feel to them. I never wanted to have to redefine myself based on who my actual blood relatives turned out to be. It was easier not knowing."

I paused, thought of what Claire would do, then boldly jumped off the dock. "Claire wrote about what happened Saint Patrick's Day."

He looked sheepish. "Even if your conception was not particularly romantic, know that I loved her."

I looked down at the half-eaten salmon on my plate, then raised my eyes until he met them. "I meant the library tower."

Trey went pale and gripped the sides of the table. He looked around and then leaned forward, dropping his voice. "That was an accident."

I leaned forward. "Was it?"

He closed his eyes. I waited, the silence repeating Claire's name in my head like a mantra. Trey leveled his gaze at me. "I have asked myself that question over and over again, and all I can tell you is as soon as it happened, I regretted ever being in that tower, ever letting my father goad me into retaliation, ever having gone to Godfrey."

"Ever having been born a Price?" I held his stare.

Trey took a deep sip of wine.

"What do you think would have happened if you'd followed Claire to California? Would your family have cut you off? Dragged you home? Found a way to take me and raise me as their own? Do you really think you could've played house without their interference? Claire faked her own death so they wouldn't get their hands on me. Just think about that for a minute."

"I don't know." He pressed his hands to his head. "I don't know."

"Having a baby at age twenty-one would have been hard enough. Having a baby without family support, harder still. Having someone try to take your baby . . ."

"My parents might have come around."

"If you and Claire did everything they wanted. Moved into their house so they could control every aspect of our lives. Let me guess. Both your kids went to Exeter, and they're expected to go to Godfrey. What would have happened the first time your father lost his temper?"

"It's not like that." Trey's voice turned sharp. "I protected my kids."

"From what I can see, you did everything your family wanted. That may have worked for Sloan, but I don't think it would have worked for Claire. And who would I have become?"

We stared at each other. Trey broke his gaze away first, picking up his knife and fork and cutting a piece of his steak. "I'd like it if we could make a space for each other in our lives. Get to know each other." He gestured between us. "Just the two of us."

"We'll see," I said. "We'll see."

* * *

I'd started helping Lauren put her inventory online. When I wanted company I joined her in the store. In a short time, Lauren had become like a favorite aunt—someone I could use as

THE SUNKEN TOWN | 223

a sounding board—and I understood why Claire trusted her. She kept what I said private.

On Sunday morning we met for brunch in town before planning to spend the day working in the bookstore. I recapped my mother's visit.

"Are you going to hate me if I tell you I knew about the letters?" she said. "I just didn't think it was my place."

"I'm starting to think there's nothing you don't know." I shook my head. "It's okay. I understand why my mother did what she did. Even if I don't like it."

I took a sip of my latte and tried to ask as casually as I could. "So, have you talked to Lucas?"

"Why does that sound like a loaded question?"

"I told him I didn't want kids and about the cottage in California. I don't think he was too happy."

She set her menu aside. "All you can do is be honest with Lucas."

"I'm trying."

"How was dinner with Trey?"

I shook my head. "I just can't get that journal entry about the football player out of my head."

"I struggled with that too, and so did Claire. I think that's why she made her decision. She didn't need the Price's money, but if she couldn't trust Trey, then what? Her grief over the loss of her parents was still right under the surface when I met her. She was handling it, but I always wondered if she found some kind of symmetry in using her fake death to bring you a new life."

"And here we are full circle."

★ ★ ★

That afternoon as I was searching the fiction shelves for the latest *New York Times* bestsellers to include in a display, Sloan walked through the door, the bell tinkling as it shut behind her. I shrank back behind the shelf and watched her approach Lauren at the register. The store was empty except for us. Lauren looked up from what she was working on and blinked. "Sloan," she said. "What brings you here?"

Trey pushed through the door behind her, slightly out of breath.

Sloan tilted her head. "I'm looking for Claire. Where can I find her?"

"Claire?" Lauren looked confused. "You mean Lindsay."

"No, I mean Claire."

Lauren looked to Trey, then walked to the door, locked it, and flipped the sign to closed. "Claire died."

"I told you," Trey said. "Let's go." He reached for Sloan's elbow. She shook him off.

"You can stop your lying now," Sloan said. "Where is she?"

Lauren folded her arms across her chest. "Claire died in a car accident on I-95 back in the spring. She's buried in a grave in California. End of story."

"I should have known her daughter would be as deceitful as she was."

"Enough, Sloan." Trey raised his voice. "I told you Claire was gone. Are you happy now?"

"I would be happy if I'd never had to hear her name again."

"Lindsay is Trey's daughter too," Lauren said.

Sloan placed her hands on her hips. "Not without a DNA test."

I stepped from behind the bookshelf to where they could see me.

Lauren shook her head and snapped. "Sloan, you know she's Trey's or you wouldn't be here. You both got the life you wanted. Claire gave up everything."

Trey stepped forward. "Claire never gave me a chance," he said to Lauren. "I would have gone with her. Stood up to my family for Claire—"

"You mean you would have thrown your life away, and my life with it," Sloan said.

Trey whipped around to face her. "I relinquished my dreams to do what was expected of me, and now it's too late to do anything else. That's hardly the role model I want to be for my children." He looked at me. "Any of my children."

I held my hands up in front of me like a shield. "I'm not looking for a replacement family," I said. "If I was, I would have asked my parents to help me find you years ago, but I never searched for Claire or you. I never wanted to."

"Then why come looking for Trey now?" Sloan asked, eyes narrowed.

I glanced at Lauren. "After reading Claire's journal entry about Saint Patrick's Day and that night after the party, I wanted to know whose genes I inherited."

Lauren pressed her lips together. She came around the counter and stood right next to me.

Sloan crossed her arms and turned to Trey. "What's she talking about?"

Trey drew his hand down his face. "It doesn't matter now." He stalked over to the history section and studied the shelf as if his life depended on finding a long-lost volume.

Sloan stared at his back, processing. "Wait a minute. Saint Patrick's Day is when Chip died," she said. "It was all anyone could talk about. Trey, tell me. Tell me now."

Trey turned to face Sloan "I was drunk," he said. "We were on the balcony. Chip was choking me. I managed to pull his hands off me, but he went over."

His voice took on a pleading quality. "It was an accident." He looked from Sloan, to Lauren, to me. "It was an accident."

"You? *You* did it? You killed Chip?" Sloan shook her head. "I told you all that fraternity crap wasn't worth it, but this? You're worse than your father."

"It was an accident! I didn't see you standing up to *your* father." Trey raised his voice to a falsetto and fluttered his eyelashes. "It was all 'Daddy this and Daddy that.'"

Sloan looked as if she'd been slapped. Trey slammed his hand against the counter. Lauren reached for my arm.

"I didn't ask for any of this." I grabbed my bag and fled.

★ ★ ★

This time it was Trey who found me sitting at the end of the dock, feet dangling in the water, staring out across the expanse of the blue pond. I didn't immediately turn when I heard his footfall on the wooden planks, but Riley rose from where he lay by my side and emitted a single questioning bark. I looked back over my shoulder to where Trey stood with his hands in his pockets and his shoulders rounded.

"I didn't want to leave things like that," Trey said. "Mind if I join you?"

I tipped my head in assent.

Trey came to where I sat, removed his shoes and socks, and eased down next to me, slipping his long, white feet into the water. A pair of iridescent blue dragonflies flitted before us and a family of ducks bobbed along the shore, tipping their tails skyward as they searched for food under the surface.

"Have you ever seen the remnants of the town under the lake?" I asked after a long moment of silence.

"Can't say that I have, but I think you'd need diving gear to get deep enough."

"I can't get it out of my head." I leaned back on my hands. The wooded slopes of the valley curved down to meet the man-made lake. A few trees still held onto their last vestige of autumn colors before baring themselves for the long winter ahead. The fall air was tinted with the tangy scent of burning leaves.

"I'm sorry about what happened back there with Sloan. She's a good person, but she can be a lot."

I shrugged. "I can't say I blame her. I didn't know if she already knew about the tower."

Trey crossed his arms. Pressed his lips together. Shook his head no.

I wiggled my toes in the water. "I told my mom I met you," I said.

"Did you," he hesitated. "Tell her?"

"No. Only you know what happened in the tower that night. And maybe you don't even know." I gazed across the rippled surface to the faraway shore. "But, for better or worse, we're all living with the consequences."

A loon called across the pond. Its mate responded somewhere off in the bushes along the shore. The water lapped gently against the dock.

"Are you here for good?" He asked.

I pushed my hair out of my face. "I haven't decided, but you can assure Sloan that I'm not looking to disrupt your family. I'm not ready to meet your kids, and I might never be. What you tell them is your choice. Your mother too. I still need time to process all this."

Trey lifted his feet from the water, letting them dry before putting his socks and shoes back on. He pressed himself up from the dock and stood, looking down at me with a solemn expression. "Don't disappear on me," he said, waiting until I nodded before striding away down the dock.

I pulled my feet back onto the dock and sat cross-legged on the well-weathered wood. Riley lay next to me, snoozing. I stroked the length of his body. My feelings about my adoption had always been calm, peaceful, untroubled. By naming me her heir, Claire changed all that.

Now I wanted to explore the mysteries hidden under the

surface. Face fears I couldn't explain. Look for a life that might have been. Begin to understand my full identity. Once, long ago, a town sat in this valley. A town where people lived and worked and played. It couldn't have been fully erased, no matter how hard they tried. I needed to know what final secrets the lake was hiding. I needed to find clarity.

CHAPTER TWENTY

Lindsay

When I learned to SCUBA dive, the kelp forests under the ocean's surface shifted from a source of terror to comfort. Suspended weightless in the cold Pacific waters, the kelp assured me which direction was up and provided anchor for the surges that swelled and tried to push me into the rocky shore.

First thing in the morning, I loaded the rented SCUBA gear into the canoe and paddled to drop anchor at the approximate location of the drowned town. Lone Loon Pond was not that deep, and any town remnants would be within my diving reach. I turned on my air, checked my regulator, and spit in my mask. After taking one last look at the serene landscape, knowing I would never again see it the same way, I slipped backward into the lake. I knew better than to dive without a buddy, but if Claire could act alone, I could as well.

The water chilled my exposed skin outside the wetsuit, but my core was warm. I steadied my breathing, unnaturally loud in the absence of other sounds, noted the time, and started my descent to the bottom, equalizing my ears along the way. Having only dived in the cold, dark waters of the Pacific pushed by tidal surges, the lake's stillness and crystalline visibility was a welcome change. I could see a fair distance in every direction and rotated slowly, checking the compass bearings. The sun filtered through the first several feet of water, illuminating floating particles like dust motes in a shaft of sunlight, and everything had that slight green sheen. A school of silver minnows darted past, and scum-covered stumps from felled trees paved the lake floor.

I finished my descent and swam in a determined line to the coordinates of the original town. Tree stumps, downed branches, decaying leaves, and boulders covered the bottom of the lake. Trout hid in the shadows, darting for cover as I kicked my way past. After a few minutes, a stone wall like the ones that still defined New England property lines materialized. My heartbeat increased. I swam above it following its algae-covered spine. Soon the remnants of building foundations appeared. An eerie reminder of all that once occupied this spot. The absence of any noise outside of my own Darth Vader breathing made me claustrophobic.

I kept swimming, following the underwater streets that people once walked, and then my breath caught. Headstones were taking shape in the green-hued water. Not one headstone, multiple headstones. A graveyard. I floated to the closest marker. Everything important was supposed to have been moved. The families should have had their ancestors relocated to a cemetery they could visit. I wondered if anyone knew who the graves belonged to or even remembered they were here, stifled under leagues of water.

My breath quickened to the verge of hyperventilating. If I wasn't careful, I would run out of air. I shut my eyes for a moment and focused on taking slow, regular breaths, not letting my anxiety spiral, then checked my air gauge. It was lower, but I still had time.

Most of the headstones were simple markers, but in the middle of the watery graveyard stood a larger family crypt that drew me. I wiped my bare hand across the stone surface, clearing the layer of scum from the writing etched in the marble. I stopped breathing—the single most dangerous act when SCUBA diving.

Carved in a simple script was a capital *W*. I traced my finger through its worn marble groove and then continued writing in the water—the letter *I*, through the peaks of the *L*s, to the second *I*, the *A*, the *M*, and ending with the *S*—the curves of the letters I had written all my life flowing from my finger. The water gave my hand an alien hue. I forced myself to inhale and exhale, not wanting Claire's charade to come true a generation later.

I imagined Claire on that early morning in May. The sun not even up yet. No fear of swimming across the lake. No fear of what was under the surface. No fear of her unknown future. It would have been so dark and cold in the water. Disorienting. She could have easily been committing herself to her real death, and me to mine. I closed my eyes. I'd never questioned who my parents were, and I still didn't. But now I also realized that I was as much a product of them as I was of the choices Claire and Trey made that led me to become a Williams.

In the utter darkness behind my eyelids, the cool water caressed my cheeks and my raspy, mechanical breath reminded me of a patient on life support. I squeezed my eyes shut even tighter and imagined Claire swimming to me from across the graveyard of headstones. Her long hair flowed behind her like streamers. She was barely in her twenties and wore the running clothes from that fateful morning. Her feet bare. When she reached me, she extended her hand. I knew what she needed.

I removed my regulator from my mouth and offered it to her. She took it and breathed from my tank. A symphony of bubbles floated to the surface around her. She gave me back the mouthpiece. I inhaled and exhaled. We continued this way, buddy breathing, alternating with the regulator, sharing my tank, staring into matching eyes. I'd been in this lake before with her. Cradled warm and suspended in her belly. I looked up. The surface was unreachable on a single breath of air.

Light bent into the lake from the sun shining above, casting its rays to the remains of the sunken town. I imagined walls growing from the forgotten foundations, roofs closing over buildings to protect interiors, frames filling in with windows and doors—the ghostly forms of the structures that once made up the town solidifying and redefining themselves to their former glory. One by one, now solid, the buildings untethered themselves from the lake bottom and floated gently to the surface— the schoolhouse, the post office, the hardware store, the people's homes, the church with its pointing steeple—rising up out of the lake and into the heavens for all the world to see.

It was impossible to speculate all the ways my life would have been different if I had not been adopted. It was also impossible to know if I would have been better off not learning the truth. Claire forced me on a journey I never planned to take, but if it weren't for her choices I would not have had the life I had. Claire took one last breath from my tank and then handed the regulator back to me. She sprang off the bottom and torpedoed to the surface of Lone Loon Pond, her hands clenched protectively against her womb. The bubbles from my breath floated after her. She did not look back.

The Inca believed that certain spots on the earth have energy vortices, Machu Picchu being one. I'd wished for clarity on a Peruvian stone that fit into the palm of my hand. Carried it on my journey, and returned it to the Incan Gods at the apex of my hike.

I pressed my hand to the clean W etched on the crypt. Claire had sacrificed everything to protect me, and then with her death presented me with the new life she had built for herself. I had been given the opportunity to see what my other life might have been like. To have had a different family. A different mother. And a different father.

I had a farmhouse and garden to learn to care for in Maine. I had a cottage with a red door and a jewelry studio waiting for me in California. And I had a dog to accompany me to both homes. I removed my palm from the solid marble of the crypt. The remains of the sunken town returned to their former abandoned state.

I reached for my air gauge. The needle was just touching the red zone. Normally, my instinct would have been to bolt to the surface, but all my hours of emergency training took over. My vision narrowed to that of my watch and the depth meter, and I slowed my ascent to let the nitrogen dissipate from my blood stream. At my last precautionary safety stop fifteen feet from the surface, I hung suspended. Just three minutes to wait. I looked up. The sun's rays reached to me through the water like a kaleidoscope. Even if I ran out of air in my tank, I would safely reach the surface.

KAREN NELSON is the author of the novel *The Sunken Town* and the co-founder of the nonprofit Writing By Writers. During her long career in nonprofits, she has protected open space, funded cancer research, trained people to complete endurance events, and helped writers bring their work into the world. When not organizing writing workshops, she can be found hiking with her dog, reading, traveling, experimenting in the kitchen, and hosting dinner parties. She writes for various publications and is currently at work on her next novel.

ACKNOWLEDGMENTS

This novel started many years ago when I found myself in the home of a woman I didn't know, who stepped out for a moment, never to return. Bringing this story from my imagination to the page is the result of many people who have supported my writing over the last thirty years.

I would like to thank Vicki DeArmon, Julia Park Tracey, Maureen Jennings, and the rest of the team at Sibylline Press for seeing something in this manuscript and for giving *The Sunken Town* a home. I believe fully in the work of small independent presses, and I couldn't be more thrilled to be published by these incredibly smart women.

To Pam Houston, who before becoming my friend and business partner, started as my brilliant writing teacher. In the twenty plus years since I met her, no one has ever been able to see where a story wants to go, and give the exact advice needed for how to get there, as well as she can. This book would never have been written without her and the PAMFAs.

To all the PAMFAs for their friendship, encouragement, and support. I would especially like to thank Cynthia Newberry Martin, Lesley Dahl, Susan von Konsky, Patricia Smith, Melanie Simonich, Peggy Sarjeant, Karen Laborde, Katherine Ellis, Tami Anderson, and Kae Penner-Howell for all the writing retreats, walks, chats, great food, and literary friendships. Collectively, they have read more versions and pages than any of us probably care to count.

To Richard Russo for being my first serious writing teacher and for teaching me how to read like a writer.

To Richard Bausch for tricking me into starting what turned out to be Claire's story, and causing me to dust off that novel sitting in my drawer. And to all the faculty who have come through

Writing By Writers. I have earned a degree a thousand times over learning from all of you.

To Joshua Mohr and Samantha Dunn, who have not only taken the time to read my work and share endless amounts of wisdom with me, but who are my writing cheerleaders. Thank you for all the love and laughs. It means the world to me.

To Cynthia Newberry Martin, who is the kind of friend every writer needs. Thank you for listening patiently to my every waking thought, for endlessly dissecting scenarios with me, and for showing me nothing but encouragement and kindness. Cindy's determination inspires me to keep my writing going forward, even when I don't want to.

To Teresa Brewer for letting me believe their Saint Helena home is my own private writer's retreat.

To my parents, Ann and Warren Nelson, who always nurtured my love of reading and writing. When I told my mother my book was being published, her response was, "Uh oh. Are your father and I in it?"

To my dog, Rusty, who sat patiently by my side while I wrote, and listened without judgement every time I read the novel aloud to him.

And to my husband, Mike Weber, for his unconditional support of my writing. He never once said I was crazy. At least not for continuing to write for all these years.

BOOK GROUP QUESTIONS

1. Although Lindsay is adopted, she and her adoptive mother, Grace, have many characteristics in common. Throughout the novel, Lindsay also discovers traits she shares with Claire and Trey. What do you think the role of nurture vs. nature plays in who a person becomes?

2. Claire goes to very drastic measures to keep the Price family from finding out about Lindsay's birth. Was it worth it? What do you think would have happened if the Price family found out? What would you have done in Claire's situation? What about Trey's?

3. Many characters including Claire, Trey, Grace and Lindsay are keeping secrets. When is it appropriate to keep a secret and when is it not?

4. The title The Sunken Town refers to the remnants of the town hidden beneath Lone Loon Pond, but it also could be a larger metaphor. What do you think The Sunken Town represents?

5. Lindsay is not interested in having children. At one point her mother, Grace, tells her "Too many generations of women were expected to be wives and mothers. I'm happy that you're of a generation who can choose." Do you agree with this?

6. Lindsay never gets to meet her birth mother Claire, but after her death, Lindsay learns about Claire through her home, friends and journal. What does Lindsay learn? What do you think the people and objects you leave behind would say about you?

7. Both Claire and Lindsay experience the cultural differences between California and Maine. What are these and what distinctions have you noticed when traveling between different regions of the country?

8. At the end of the book, Lindsay says, "I had a farmhouse and garden to learn to care for in Maine. I had a cottage with a red door and a jewelry studio waiting for me in California. And I had a dog to accompany me to both homes." What do you think she should do next?

9. There are several Godfrey College traditions mentioned in the novel. Are they specific to Godfrey? What were your college's traditions?

10. The Inca believed that certain spots on the earth have energy vortices including Machu Picchu. Do you believe this? Have you ever experienced a phenomenon that you couldn't explain?

For other fabulous Sibylline Digital First titles, please visit
www.sibyllinepress.com

Made in United States
North Haven, CT
26 March 2025

67236579R00150